THE SEVEN MAGNIFICENT MIND-SETS OF SUCCESS

Your Successes May Only Be.....

.....An Adventure Away

THE SEVEN MAGNIFICENT MIND-SETS OF SUCCESS

ADVENTURES WITH THE MAGNIFICENT MIND-SET MAN

RUSS HAMBLIN

Copyright © 2023 Russ Hamblin.

All rights reserved. No part of this book may be reproduced, stored, or transmitted by any means—whether auditory, graphic, mechanical, or electronic—without written permission of both publisher and author, except in the case of brief excerpts used in critical articles and reviews. Unauthorized reproduction of any part of this work is illegal and is punishable by law.

ISBN: 979-8-89031-279-2 (sc)
ISBN: 979-8-89031-280-8 (hc)
ISBN: 979-8-89031-281-5 (e)

Because of the dynamic nature of the Internet, any web addresses or links contained in this book may have changed since publication and may no longer be valid. The views expressed in this work are solely those of the author and do not necessarily reflect the views of the publisher, and the publisher hereby disclaims any responsibility for them.

One Galleria Blvd., Suite 1900, Metairie, LA 70001
1-888-421-2397

CONTENTS

Preface vii

Chapter 1   An Unexpected Reunion..1
Chapter 2   A Typical Expedition Begins...17
Chapter 3   A Mysterious Visitor's Definition Of Success 33
Chapter 4   A Timely Introduction..47
Chapter 5   A Better Path: Mind-Set Technologies 64
Chapter 6   Mind-Set 1: You Were Born to Win..............................70
Chapter 7   Mind-Set 2: Understand And Nullify Entropy 79
Chapter 8   Mind-Set 3: Be F.A.I.R. to Yourself 88
Chapter 9   Mind-Set 4: Be *Turned-Out* and Win.........................100
Chapter 10   Mind-Set 5: Improve Your Personal Weather Forecast ... 119
Chapter 11   The Mountain, The Weather,
                   And The Magnificent Mind-Set Man........................ 133
Chapter 12   Mind-Set 6: Never Give Up!..144
Chapter 13   Mind-Set: 7 Grow From Base to Grace...................... 152
Chapter 14   The Rescue on Bokan Mountain 167
Chapter 15   The Final Awakening...178

About the Book.. 183

PREFACE

This book has been a long and arduous, but rewarding journey for me. As with most authors, it has evolved into both a literal and at times transcendental catharsis of the many experiences, successes, and failures that I've sustained and endured during the past 64 years of my adventurous and sometimes tumultuous life. And it has ended up being one of the most worthwhile things that I've ever undertaken.

Not too many years ago, I was struggling through some of the darkest and most frustrating times of my life. Within a period of two and a half of years, I endured a difficult divorce after 35 years of marriage, adjusted to a new job, suddenly lost both my second wife and my mother, and was striving to recover from a serious gambling addiction. To cope with these challenges, I dug deep and established several personal and faith-based goals to live more responsibly and with an upstanding purpose. Despite my stalwart convictions though, I was still battered with the pangs of my strong and daunting gambling addiction, mostly because it fed my alter-ego of a slick, care-free, itinerant swashbuckler who could cast freedom to the wind and let every exciting roll of the dice decide his fate.

With the passage of time, the abyss of personal tragedies and destruction that I had dug for myself became too deep. So one day, I started to get the demons out of my being, in the open, and down on paper where I could read and reread them. And only then when I was confronted with them in their entirety did I begin to see them for the ghosts, lies, and specters that they truly were. With those curtains finally drawn, my own deep reflection and soul-searching began, and my written words slowly coalesced and allowed me to see where I was headed in life, who I was becoming, where that might lead, and forced me to gruelingly climb the upward path back to personal righteousness. It showcased who I had become over too many years – and I neither liked that person nor wanted to be around him anymore. And at that juncture, I finally began to understand that my past failures did not have to dictate who I would be in the future.

Beyond my own words and thoughts, I greatly benefitted from the holy scriptures and felt that the inspiration, wisdom, and strength that I discovered within, was the real truth behind my many prayers answered. They say God helps those that help themselves and indubitably, it was the dawn of that reality finally becoming luminous in my being, that spurred me on to overcome the nettles of my past and rebuild my future with the soundest of indestructible armor.

Coincident with my convictions, I was thereafter very fortunate to find the love of my life, Julie. We were married and she has lovingly supported me with my challenges and encouraged me to continue on with my writing. And it was through that dedication that I began realizing that the many sentences and chapters of my life and struggles that I had been writing about constituted nothing short of a book – a treatise that could perhaps be used to help others. With that new sense of accomplishment and volition, I embraced my new-found vision and knew that my former hole of personal destruction was now buried by the very voluminous shovels of my words and life-long mission now immortalized in this book.

Through the course of writing The Seven Magnificent Mind-sets of Success, Adventures with the Magnificent Mind-set Man,, I must confess that I was aware from the very start that the last thing this world needs is another success-oriented motivational book. That being said, the idea behind this work is to present a partly fictional story of how a spiritual journey helped the books protagonist Roger Hunt both find himself and overcome his struggles and challenges through a unique system of mental disciplines that were given to him. It presents this philosophy by taking the reader on a thrilling adventure to a remote island of the Alaska's wilderness, part of my ramblings as an actual geologist that has taken me to Egypt and even outer Mongolia.

In the end, The Seven Magnificent Mind-sets of Success, Adventures with the Magnificent Mind-set Man is a book about second chances in life and that it is never too late to make changes. In my own words from my own hell and back and as a takeaway to anyone who has or is struggling with personal challenges of any kind, always remember that *the roads that lead to the greatest successes in life are often paved with the foundational stones of many setbacks, disappointments, and failures that one must experience in order to gain the perspective needed to grow and attain sustainable joy and happiness.*

You can become the successful person you always wanted to be, and the time to begin, is now! I hope this book may help you on your path!

Take Care and Make Good Things Happen!
Russell D. Hamblin, R.G.
February 2022

CHAPTER 1

AN UNEXPECTED REUNION

On an ordinary wintery Tuesday late afternoon in early February 2016, Roger Hunt's life was about to change from the ordinary to the extraordinary. He was totally unaware that within the next ten minutes he would be forced to change his thinking from *how frantic and crazy life had been for me lately*; to, *will I make it through the night without being stranded on a dangerous and lonely two-lane highway, miles from civilization*. Also that night, Roger would be faced with a 10-year- old question that had been growing and tormenting him of late, *do I continue in my same mediocre-successful life with an ever-growing temptation to fall back into my destructive habits, or will I finally keep my promise that I once made to an old friend who I barely knew, a mentor who once enlightened me, and a rescuer who tried to save me?*

Roger was 58 years-young, or so he thought. Like your average middle-aged man, he was successful in some ways but had failed in others. Each and every day of his mostly-ordinary and sometimes eventful life, from sun up to sun down, he would approach new challenges and opportunities in an over-optimistic and cavalier manner, always trying to bite off more than he could chew with respect to work and other things in his busy schedule, which oftentimes lead to undue stress and anxieties that he did not need in his life.

In his own mind, Roger was many things; a husband, a father, a grandfather, a fairly successful independent environmental geologist and small business-owner, and a man of deep faith and conviction to his Christian values. Roger also knew that he was a recovering gambling addict with many ups and downs in his abilities to finally overcome this debilitating habit.

While Roger was driving north from Elko, Nevada, to Boise, Idaho, that pivotal night in his 2012 black Tundra pickup on that remote highway, he slowly began to realize that he was running low on sunlight and fuel. Daily temperatures the last few days in the region averaged from 20°F to 25°F and weather conditions that Tuesday afternoon were fair to partly cloudy. Recent snowfalls produced just a white veneer in the valleys, up to one foot of snow in the higher areas, and up to two feet of fresh snowpack in the surrounding 8,500-foot peaks of the Northern Basin and Range mountains of Northern Nevada and Southern Idaho.

With limited staff, he had been on the road more often than he wanted, taking work matters into his own hands. So during this wintery week, Roger found himself driving long hours, starting early in the morning and going late into the night. During the morning hours of this day, Roger completed field training with a newly-hired associate on a contaminated property located in Carlin, Nevada. Later in the morning and early afternoon, Roger found lunch and a Wi-Fi hot spot at a McDonalds in Elko, Nevada and kept himself busy on his razor-thin HP laptop completing a couple of proposals for his clients, and then on his iPhone conversing with new clients and scheduling several projects. He mistakenly thought he had a glimmer of hope to reach Boise, Idaho before sundown to meet another property developer interested in turning an oily-stained wrecking yard into a brand new convenience gasoline store, which had many environmental contamination issues to resolve. But not too long after being on the road, Roger also began to realize that reaching the capitol city of Idaho before dusk, was probably a futile effort.

Out of frustration, Roger began slowly shaking his head and gripping his iPhone tightly in his right hand as he firmly grasping the steering wheel with his left hand. He started to realize that he was falling back into his old stress-related habits of over-scheduling and under planning; trying to cram too much into one day and not getting enough rest while traveling for business. And then, to make matters worse, Roger suddenly remembered his hectic schedule over the next couple of days. One that would put him on a sixhour flight from Boise to Anchorage, Alaska tomorrow so that he could hold a proposal meeting with a new mining client on the following day, Thursday. All this before returning home on Friday to spend a restful and romantic weekend with his best friend and wife of twelve years, Julie in their warm and cozy log home in the Salt Lake Valley, Utah.

Lately, Roger was trying harder lately to set time management goals to keep himself from getting into stressful working situations, being on the road and out of town for too many consecutive days, and putting work before his more important family relationships. These were some of the things that led to led to many selfish habits and eventually to a failed first marriage nearly twenty years ago with the mother of his four children. Now he was trying to remind himself to do everything he could to correct such issues in his current marriage with Julie, whom he considered to be the love of his life.

With the potential to turn the day into a complete disaster, Roger also hadn't fueled up in Elko, like he knew he should have. Because he hadn't paid attention to the warning signs, either, Roger suddenly realized he was indeed, running out of gas. He also just realized that he was miles away from any rural town in Southwestern Idaho— or any town for that matter, with a gas station.

Roger and Julie affectionately called their trusty friend, *the Black Pearl*, because of its shiny-black color and since it had been a very reliable work vehicle for Roger throughout the years, even though it was quite thoroughly field-worn with nearly 100,000 miles on the odometer in only 4 ½ years of hard driving. This nickname also fit well for the truck as Roger would often disappear with it, driving off into the night for out-of-town business trips, according to Julie.

Keeping one eye on the fuel gauge and the other eye on the indicator showing he had about eight to ten miles of road to travel before reaching empty, Roger did some crude math in his head. He didn't like the numbers he was coming up with. He also kept a lookout for highway signs that would reveal how far he was to the nearest town. Finally, around the next turn on the lonely road, he saw a shotgun-pitted highway mileage sign that read: fifty miles to a small town called, Mountain Home, Idaho and ninety-eight miles to Boise. Roger knew that the next few minutes would be critical for his comfort and safety.

In near panic, Roger started looking for nearby farmhouses. None. He saw no homes and no cars. The sunlight was decreasing, and he was running out of time, gas, and luck. A moment later Roger spotted a dusty, unpaved road to his right with a cattle guard at its entrance, indicating a possible off-road ranch or nearby farm house. He slowed the Black Pearl down and began debating in his mind whether or not to take the dirt path. *If I take the road, would it lead to a farmhouse with a fuel tank? Or, would I be better off trying to flag down the next driver heading north and catch a ride with a Good Samaritan to the nearest town, get gas in a can, and catch anther ride back to the Black Pearl with another Good Samaritan?* The thought of hitchhiking was a scary proposition for Roger; he was afraid of meeting a criminal looking to rob a vulnerable traveler on a lonely highway. Many other dangerous scenarios began running through his mind.

Roger sighed, *How am I going to get myself out of this mess?*

The latter option seemed risky since this road had not produced another vehicle for over thirty minutes, and it looked like he had only about twenty minutes of daylight left, at best.

Thinking that he may have seen a semblance of a structure, maybe a farmhouse, off in the distance a mile or two, Roger chose to go off the main road to search for an immediate payoff.

He thought, *I'll take this road for two, maybe three miles, and if I can't find that farmhouse with a gas tank, then I'll have enough fuel to get back to the main highway and go to Plan B.*

A leap of faith? Maybe. But that little voice inside of him said, *You're doing the right thing, everything will work out.*

Just seek and you will find, borrowing a familiar verse from the Bible, with the idea he would apply a scintilla of positive attitude. He had learned those positive mental attitude tactics as a younger man as he feasted upon the bestselling book *The Amazing Results of Positive Thinking,* by the late Dr. Norman Vincent Peale.

Be optimistic and go for it, Roger! he told himself as he began his adventure on the dirt road. *Uphill or windy, dirty or bumpy, this path will either produce or bust,* Roger told himself.

Turn after turn; one mile, two miles, two and three quarter miles, and no results: no house, no fuel tanks; nothing of substance was seen.

One more turn coming up, and if there's no sign of a house, I swear I will turn around and go back before I go too far with no possibility of returning to the main highway, he thought.

As Roger slowly came around the turn, he finally spotted an old, rickety, relatively large, two-story ranch house. As he approached the derelict structure, Roger noted that it was built of dusty-brown logs with white chinking. The aged home appeared to be dark, abandoned, and dilapidated. *Apparently nobody's home—maybe not for years, by the looks of things,* Roger thought to himself.

Roger parked and quickly got out of the Black Pearl. He put on his dark brown Carhartts® brand field coat and grey wool gloves to keep him warm. Then immediately, he started looking around for any sign of life—and maybe if he was lucky, a gas tank.

After a few moments of surveying the property, Roger decided that the former inhabitant of this old ranch house could not be too bad of a person, based on the copious amounts of colorful rocks lining the driveway, walkway, and landscaping areas. He saw large rocks up to three to four feet in diameter, medium-sized rocks, and fist-sized rocks; broke-up geodes with large crystals of clear quartz, vibrant smoky quartz, and deep purple amethyst. Then he noticed other large rocks of several varieties of granites: extra-large crystalline rocks called pegmatites, granite-like metamorphic gneisses of several varieties, and curious-looking migmatities with white squiggly-looking veins of milky quartz and rectangular-feldspar.

Roger also noted several large, garden-sized rocks with yellow and red iron ore, including limonite and hematite, and green and blue copper ore, known in science as malachite and azurite. Over to the extreme left, he noticed petrified wood fragments ranging from 2 feet to over 4 feet long; there were also common fossils from all over the world and from each of the three geologic eras, including large, one-foot-diameter and coiled ammonites and trilobites from the Early Paleozoic; younger, uncoiled ammonites and dinosaur bones typically from the Late Mesozoic; and mastodon and wooly mammoth bones from the late Cenozoic, the current Geologic Period.

Then there was a section of rocks that looked noticeably and strangely familiar to Roger, including granitic rocks, stained with red streaks, which had the appearance of hematite. A thought popped into his mind that he had likely seen rocks similar to these, nearly ten years ago during a ten-day field investigation on a remote island off the coast of the Pacific Ocean near Ketchikan, Alaska. As he recalled that mysterious and beautiful place, he sensed a shadow of glum and guilt overcoming him to a point of an unexplainable feeling of melancholy.

Those feelings of depression slowly were replaced with a sense of hope and comfort as those familiar crimson rocks also reminded him of an unforgettable adventure that he experienced in splendor-filled mountainous island where he had once worked for several days. Roger recalled that he had learned so many profound lessons that he should have more fully applied to his life. This hope started to fade again back into feelings of sadness as Roger began to reminisce and admit to himself, that; there were so *many valuable and profound perspectives that were offered me from those experiences. The readings and essays from that visionary avatar-like mentor who taught me many so important lessons. Those concepts and new mind-sets; if I had only embraced them applied them, and lived them, they could have helped me! Not only could they have made me more successful in life, but they could have strengthened me to resist the temptations to gamble and to occasionally fall back into the darkness of my old ways.*

Suddenly, Roger came to himself and began to appreciate his surroundings a little more. *The simplicity and beauty of the owner's display from a geologist's point of view,* Roger realized, *These were not just rocks laying around in a random fashion in a rock-hound's junk yard or a man that was trying to open up his own rock shop for profit.*

Roger continued his admiration with further vocal accolades. *This man isn't a rock hound or novice at all, He's a professional. This is some kind of professor or miner who had a strange way of adorning his dilapidated ranch with earth treasures from around the world.* Roger would have bet that this man had retired here and wanted to relish his professional memories while relaxing on the range. *The best of two worlds for this old guy,* Roger projected in admiration.

This is my kind of guy! Roger gawked for a few precious moments, almost forgetting about his painful omissions and commissions of his past, as well as his current and potentially dangerous predicament.

Then, he suddenly came to himself again, but this time in a more urgent and practical manner; he remembered his present situation and his need for fuel, as he noticed the sun setting quickly to the west with a majestic combination of thin clouds turning orange and red and getting redder and lower and lower by the minute.

Back to getting myself out of trouble. Roger gazed about for any sign of farm tanks, and shouted, *any tanks?* And then he spotted two 500gallon brown steel tanks resting on old wooden stilts.

Ah-hah! There they are! Roger shouted with joy, thinking he was nearly out of his predicament.

The stilts were probably from the 1950s, exhibiting chipping white paint. They were about five feet tall, and were located in the back next to a rundown barn and decaying corrals. The tank to his left was labeled with a dirt-smudged *No. 2 diesel* marker, while the tank to his right was clearly labeled, *unleaded gasoline.* He knocked on the gasoline tank with his fist to detect if there was any appreciable amount of fuel inside. From the sound that echoed back, it appeared that the gasoline tank was about half-full. *That's encouraging!* Roger barked.

Roger, knowing the difference in smell of the two fuels, was also gladdened to catch a fresh sent of gasoline coming from some minor spillage on the ground under the tank marked gasoline, guessing that the fuel also wasn't too old to be of good use for his immediate needs.

Good and plenty Roger bragged; two additional good signs of promise for the aid he needed.

There was only one problem: the dispenser nozzles attached to the tanks were both locked. No horses, no cattle, no rancher! And both tanks were secured with new, high-grade metal padlocks— the more expensive kind—and they did not appear to have either a combination or a keyhole. Roger concluded they must have been electronic or required some kind of magnetic devise to unlock. *Of course, I don't have bolt cutters!* Roger frowned in frustration.

He continued thinking. *Hmm. Strange. State-of-the-art locks at an old ranch house that apparently hasn't been inhabited in ten or more years. Where are my dang bolt cutters when I need them?*

So now what? There was no one around to hear his call for help. But he had to try, regardless. *Hello!* No reply, only dead silence.

After a couple of slow-moving moments without an answer, Roger started back to the house to try the other side of the property for help.

Suddenly, to his amazement, he abruptly met a mysterious bearded old man standing about 5 foot, 9 inches in height, with light reddish-blonde hair—thick and wavy, medium in length, with no sign of balding. He was lean, probably between 155 to 165 pounds of a well-built frame of sheer muscle, clothed in a clean brown vest over a red-checkered plaid long-sleeve shirt and light brown field pants, with hiking boots that looked old and well broken in. His face showed age but was more calloused than wrinkled. Whether a rancher, a geologist, or a world explorer, this man was old, but he was far from worn-out.

Whaddaya want? The old-timer's voice both gravelly and sharp. He puffed on an old, unlit, and empty corncob pipe protruding out of the left side of his mouth. *I said, whaddaya want?* This time the words came out in a hissing manner out the right side of his mouth with a loud, piercing whisper.

Roger just stood there in amusement for a split second, peering at the professor-like fossil of a man, who was also apparently an old rancher due to his place of residence.

A third time the old man said, *What do you want, young man? How can I help you?*

Umm, ga-ga-gas! Gas! Roger's stuttering was always a problem for him when he was startled or caught by surprise.

After a deep breath and a short clearing of his throat, Roger, eventually collected himself and crafted an answer. *I-I was wondering if you can help out a needy traveler and fellow geologist with some gas. I'm all but out, and I'm nowhere near a gas station.*

The old-timer responded with a chuckle. *Geologist? What makes you think I'm a geologist, young man?*

Your rocks! Roger replied. *Your rocks and the way you present them. You have a system of display that screams of order and knowledge, like you are displaying a story of your profession or present a condensed geologic history of the world.*

Roger then shifted his tone to be even more flattering. *We geologists can tell the difference, you know, between a real geologist and a common rock hound.*

The old timer began slowly laughing out of the right side of his mouth. *Huh, huh, huh. Geologist I am, I guess. Yeah! I guess I can spare a few gallons of gas for your truck; after all, you are a student of mine you know.*

Roger slightly cocked his head, but did not even try to figure out the meaning of that comment; he was just glad to be getting the gas he needed. He thanked the old timer profusely with a cheerful smile. He was also anxious to get back on his way to the nearest gas station in Mountain Home, Idaho and get the Black Pearl fully gassed-up for the rest of his journey to Boise, where he would spend the night and resume his demanding work schedule in the morning. Knowing that he had missed his evening appoint for that night with minimal regret, he was truly thankful for the help he was receiving.

The old-timer smiled with pride as Roger stood speechless, not knowing what to say in response. His grey eyebrows lifted and his mouth opened again as if he wanted to say more to Roger, but did not. Roger momentarily wondered if the old man expected him to play along with a reply of that sounded like, *Oh yes! Professor Jones, I was one of your former students at the university*, or, oh yeah, *I was a past geologic acolyte of yours at the old mine site*, or something similar. But Roger refused to play along with what he concluded was just a spontaneous joke.

Looking disappointed that Roger was not playing along with his convivial sparring, the old man reached into his right front pocket and pulled out a metallic card. It was rectangular-shaped, about one and a half inches wide by three inches long. The card had a shiny violet color and was blank, not showing any form of markings or magnetic strip. Roger could not quite remember when he had seen such a lock-and-key device before, but he was sure that he had, maybe even within the last five to ten years.

Without saying a word, the old-timer turned and started walking over to his fuel tanks.

Wow, thanks! Roger said. Then added, *Pretty cool-looking key card you have there, sir. What kind of metal is that*?

The old man then grumbled, *You know what it is young man!*

Okay? I do? Roger replied. *I actually have no idea sir. By the way, I'm Roger, Roger Hunt.* The old man seemed to already know his name. *Yes Hunt, I know you!* Roger thought he was just being sarcastic, since he had refused to play along with the old-timer's apparent student–professor joke.

What's your name, sir? Roger asked.

Billy! Roger instantaneously flinched, being surprised with Billy's gruff response.

Billy? Billy what?

But Billy didn't share his last name at that moment. He just proceeded toward the tank with no further chatter.

As Billy approached the tank, he waved his little metallic card near the lock and it immediately unlocked the pump nozzle from the tank, just like clock-work. Then he yelled out for Roger to pull his truck next to the tank so the dispenser hose would reach.

As he lifted his pump nozzle toward Roger's tank, Billy gave him a second look as if he wanted to clarify his student–professor comment, but he just gave Roger a subtle half-smile and started pumping without saying another word. When about five or six gallons were dispensed, Billy, disengaged the metal trigger switch, hung-up the hose at the tank, and then relocked the nozzle into the tank holder with another wave of his somewhat *familiar-looking key card.*

There you go, Mr. Hunt!

Thanks, Mr. Billy! Can I pay you for the gas? Roger tried to hand Billy a $20 bill.

No! Again Roger was surprised at his sharp and impatient reply. *I don't want your money! What I want is for you to pay attention to me and my advice, once and for all! I want you to do what you know you need to do with your life, to be a success and help others along the way. I want you to apply what you learned from me years ago on the mountain.*

On the mountain? Roger asked. *What mountain are you talking about, Professor Billy? Or whoever you are?*

Not meaning to be disrespectful, but maybe a little facetious, Roger tried his best to play along with a smile on his face and expecting a smile back. But a smile was not reciprocated from the old man. Instead, he peered into Billy's serious and steadfast eyes, which mesmerized Roger and made him feel as if he were in a daze or a momentary dream with a flashback to mysterious wilderness area Roger know immediately.

Roger turned away for a moment to blink and shake his head to get back into his full senses and figure out how to reply, but when he looked back towards the old man, Billy was suddenly gone. Not just walking-away-gone—no! He was gone-gone, in a flash! It was as if Billy had never been there.

That was weird! Where the devil he go? Roger began calling out, *Billy? Billy?*

By this time the night was dark at the ranch. Roger quickly got into the glove box of the Black Pearl and searched frantically until he found his flashlight. He began to shine it towards the tank, the house, the barn, the corral, and then the rock garden. But there was no sign of Billy. It was as if the whole encounter was only a dream.

At this point, not knowing whether he just imagined this experience or not, Roger decided to quickly get back into the Black Pearl, start it up, and see if he actually had the fuel. Seeing that the tank registered between one-quarter and one-half full, Roger decided to dismiss this experience, count his blessings, and be back on his way to Boise. So, off he drove, back down the cold, dusty, and winding path with his lights on high beam, heading to the main highway and back on his way to civilization and a real gas station.

As he pulled back on to the main highway, Roger sighed deeply with relief and appreciation. He was grateful he had gotten the help he needed, even if he could not explain all the details of the experience. Roger was just glad to have the fuel and to be back on firm pavement again. He vowed not to tell a soul of his strange experience with the *Professor Billy* since he was sure no one would ever believe him anyway. Such feelings of self-defeat and self-doubt were other constant problems Roger experienced throughout his life.

Although Roger had often prided himself as being an ambitious, hard-working independent geological and environmental consultant, and the CEO of his small company, Innovative Environmental Solutions (IES), he knew that he could have been much more successful in his life. He also knew that joy and happiness was something he had failed to fully experience on a regular basis. Even though his work-related adventures over the last thirty years, which included conducting scientific and environmental studies on high-risk real estate acquisitions throughout the United States and in many far off places, seemed somewhat financially satisfying and oftentimes exciting, he knew in his heart that he was somehow missing the big picture of what life was really all about. Roger always seemed to be searching for better solutions to his internal struggles, but finding those solutions was elusive.

Roger hadn't driven more than a few hundred feet on the two-lane Idaho State Highway 51 before he was startled to see the figure of a man standing in his lane with his right hand elevated in the halt position.

What's that! Startled, Roger came to a sudden braking stop within only fifteen feet of the figure. With his lights still on high beam, Roger quickly realized that it was the same old distinguished gentleman, his fellow geologist, who had saved him from being stranded.

Dr. Billy? Roger was stunned and amazed that he did not hit the old man. He quickly rolled down his side window and said. *Are you crazy, old man? I almost hit you! What do you want from me?*

Hunt! You know who I am! You know what I taught and revealed to you ten years ago on Bokan Mountain.

In a flash, Roger's mind was carried back to a remote island off the southern coast of Alaska, fifty miles from civilization. That ten- day ordeal a decade ago that had often haunted him and at the same time enlightened him so much over the years.

You! You're Billy Haynes! Roger said, shaking his head in amazement. *You're that mysterious old man I met years ago on Bokan Mountain! I didn't know if you were real then, and don't know if you're real now!*

Oh I'm real alright, and you do know me! Billy said. *Now, you listen to me for the last time, Hunt! I need you to remember the importance of your experiences from the MindSet Man and record all that you learned back then: all of the signs, experiences, analogies, and dreams that I embedded into your mind. I know you remember how I saved your life at least four times during that week- and-a-half ordeal. Doesn't that prove that I am real and that your life is important; that you have a special mission to fulfill? Look at you! Look at yourself, Hunt! Are you the success you wanted to be? Are you as happy as you could be? Are you the man you wanted to be, Hunt?*

Roger began whispering under his breath while slowly shaking his head. *No, I'm not.*

What did you say, Hunt?

I said no! I am not the man I could have been! With this haunting admission, Roger began feeling sorrow and regret for his failures over the past several years. He also felt a tear or two running down the side of his cheek. He knew that he had neglected his family too many times in favor of work. He remembered allowing himself to get too self-absorbed in his own selfish desires, spending copious amounts of time on the road with a demanding job. He also realized that most of the anxieties that consumed him were related to not taking the time to enjoy life or be grateful for all of the good things the Lord had blessed him with throughout his fifty-seven years.

As Roger was absorbed with self-pity, Billy was rapidly pacing back and forth in front of the truck, shaking his head repeatedly as if he were trying to find the right words to guide Roger, as a father would guide his wayward son.

Then suddenly, Billy stopped his pacing on a dime, pointed directly at Roger, and said, *Some failure is guaranteed in this world, Hunt. But no failure has to be permanent! We can and should learn from our failures as the lessons we need to help us better prepare for success. Never forget these words, Hunt, the same words I tried to embed into your mind years ago!* Billy paused and then continued with a former quote that sounded very familiar to Roger. *Nothing good happens by itself; so if you do nothing, nothing good will happen.*

And then as Billy's eyes starred deeply into Roger's soul, he said, *So, Roger, the question you have to ask yourself, is—* Billy again paused for a few short seconds, closed one eye, cocked his head slightly, and puckered his lips. *Whatcha gunna do about it?*

Suddenly, Billy again vanished mysteriously, and Roger again found himself alone.

Roger knew he needed to get off the highway and clear his mind, so he quickly turned his pickup off the road and onto the shoulder of the highway. There, as he collected himself, Roger pondered the strange experiences he witnessed over the last several minutes. Then, the memories came hard and fast to Roger's mind. He knew Billy Haynes was that mysterious mentor who had spoken to him all those years ago about the symbols and concepts of the *Magnificent Mind-Set Man*. He began remembering the concepts he once learned; *Mind-Set Technologies, The 7 Transcending Mind-Sets of Success*, and all of the other transforming concepts that he never really fully applied to his life, the way he should have. He regretted that he never kept the *Billy Haynes Challenge* to learn, adopt and live the transcending mind-sets of success and to write his own book that could have helped him overcome his addictions and bad habits, and which could have help others as well.

Roger thought no one would ever believe his account of what happened on that remote island a decade ago. He thought he would be ridiculed if he ever tried sharing the truth about his experiences. He was afraid that rejection would cause more pain and self-doubt in his life. He knew that he could not handle any ridicule or undeserved criticism. Basically, because Roger lacked the necessary determination, courage, and faith in himself; he did nothing with the concepts he learned. Therefore, no real changes were made, no lessons were gained, no new wisdom was applied, and no book was ever written during the last ten years. As a result, he continued to struggle and even gamble a few more times, which added more stress and anxieties to his life.

As Roger reflected, he began to lament as he grabbed his iPhone and threw it onto the passenger seat of the Black Pearl. *Why didn't I do it! Why didn't I write about the teachings of Billy Haynes and the dreams and visions of The Magnificent Mind-Set Man. Why didn't I personally apply and teach those magnificent mind-sets! Why! Is still know them by heart! I can still hear the eagle's cry in my mind and in my heart!*

Roger soon became immersed in the memories of that ten-day ordeal and the experiences that should have changed his life. *I ran from that experience when I should have embraced it. Those concepts were meant to help me overcome my fears and failures and then help others. What's wrong with me? Is it too late Billy? Is it too late for me?*

Gradually, the memories of a peaceful lake, luscious fir trees, and green brush all over a beautiful mountain cliff appeared in his mind: a place he had once visited, a place of serenity, beauty, adventure, and redemption. Because of these positive thoughts, his feelings of self-pity, regret, and depression were soon replaced with peaceful and comforting emotions. The memories of the many wondrous experiences calmed his mind and soon became a remedy for his anxious regret.

Roger began reliving those experiences in his mind and the lessons, which he knew he should never forget. *Oh the majestic Bokan Mountain with its granite cliffs and the deep blue waters of Precipice Lake.* He began mumbling these words in a peaceful slumber. *Beautiful Bokan Mountain; its pools of pure and enlightening waters.* He slowly repeated these words over and over again. These thoughts and mental images continued to soothe Roger, sending him into a visionary sleep.

As Roger gradually dosed into a peaceful slumber in the Black Pearl, he began to dream and relive those challenging and beautiful experiences he endured nearly a decade ago. He remembered that when he was afraid, alone and sometimes in peril, he was protected from physical danger. He was also peacefully reminded of the knowledge he was given to help him overcome, addictions, mental stress and anger. Roger recalled that the enlightenment provided could still enable him to replace negative thoughts with positive actions. Roger was also comforted in his sleep to know that he had been endowed with wisdom and with the keys of success, which were taught to him by a stranger, a wanderer, and a true and everlasting friend. As Roger's slumber deepened, he began mumbling some wishful words. *I want to move forward this time, Billy; I still want to write my own book and change my life; I need another chance. Billy...?*

CHAPTER 2

A TYPICAL EXPEDITION BEGINS

Monday, September 25, 2006 (Expedition - Day One)

With an abrupt jolt of air turbulence, Roger suddenly awoke and found himself in a four-passenger turbine-helicopter. It took a moment, but Roger remembered he was flying to the south end of Prince of Wales Island, near Bokan Mountain, approximately 50 miles southwest of the city of Ketchikan, Alaska. Roger gazed at the front of the copter, and there was Dr. Eddie Tyler in the cockpit pilot seat; to his right in the copilot seat was Dr. Keiffer Selos. Tyler and Selos were two of several principals of Metro Metals Inc. of Anchorage, Alaska, which had hired Roger to conduct environmental and radiological studies on forested and mountainous land that included over 600 acres of mining claims on and around Bokan Mountain. Roger was in the back seat immediately behind Selos, and the seat to his left was empty. It should have been occupied by a member of his team, Dr. Kurt Brundy, assistant professor in geochemistry and geophysics at the University of Alaska, Anchorage. But the young professor had suddenly fallen ill the evening before and couldn't make the trip.

Roger had been nodding off and on during the relatively short, fifty-minute flight. He had spent many hours the previous night with Dr. Brundy in the Ketchikan hospital, who had acute appendicitis and required an emergency appendectomy overnight. Brundy's operation appeared to be successful and physicians predicted he would soon fully recover. But the surgery rendered him out of service for at least the next six weeks. As a result, Roger was forced to conduct the expedition, both the environmental and radiological studies, by himself.

The studies had to proceed during the last week of September. Prince of Wales Island typically received about 120 inches in annual precipitation, approximately 25 percent of which would fall in the month of October alone according to prognosticators. Therefore, the team thought it was expedient to get the fieldwork done before the rains came and made it difficult to complete the project.

Not as cold as the northern parts of Alaska, Prince of Wales Island had a moist, maritime climate dominated by a high-humidity type of cold. Average summer temperatures ranged from 49 to 63 degrees Fahrenheit and winter temperatures averaged from 32 to 42 degrees Fahrenheit, including about forty inches of snow. The island was relatively unknown in the world because of its low population, 90 percent of which lived in the town of Craig to the north.

The Bokan Mountain area to the south was nearly uninhabited by humans, with only hunters and fishermen visiting the area seasonally. Surprisingly, it was third largest island in the US, with only Alaska's Kodiak Island and the Big Island of Hawaii having more square miles. Densely vegetated with Douglas fir trees, black junipers, thick brush, and multi-colored wildflowers. Island fauna consisted of salmon in the rivers and varieties of wild trout in lakes, black bears, bald eagles, owls, and deer.

If the environmental team waited even one to two additional weeks to start the field expedition, they would be totally hampered by copious amounts of rain, as much as thirty inches within three to four weeks—not ideal when it comes to conducting any meaningful fieldwork. Typically, the first week of the rainy season was the worst, coming in the forms of hail, thundershowers, and gusty winds up to forty miles per hour. So the Innovative Environmental Solutions—Metro Metals Inc. team decided to proceed with the studies, with Roger taking on the environmental and radiological studies by himself.

Hunt and Brundy had met up three days earlier at the Dunn Hotel in Ketchikan, which was an old downtown-style hotel built in the early 1920s. Despite its age the hotel was well kept and maintained throughout the years. By the third week of September, the little city was practically a ghost town, since the peak of the tourist season had come to a complete halt with the departure of the last of the cruise ships. About two-thirds of the downtown area of Ketchikan were getting boarded up for the season; all the gift shops, jewelry stores, and specialized boutiques would have to wait another seven months for the scores of cruise ships to return, bringing in tens of thousands of new shoppers and tourists beginning in May the next year.

During the those three days, Hunt and Brundy were busy, hurriedly making the final plans for the next five to seven days of rigorous work on the island. Metro Metals had hired Brundy, an expert in radiation geophysics, to conduct radiological studies, while Hunt was hired as an independent environmental consultant to conduct an environmental study of the abandoned Tyler-Haynes uranium mine. The mine complex was quite active during the Cold War throughout the 1950s, 60s, 70s, and 80s. It consisted of open-pit and underground uranium mining operations and was active for about 35 years before suddenly reaching its climax with the onset of Soviet Perestroika and associated nuclear weapon cutbacks in the late 1980s.

Now, 25-plus years after the Cold War, with virtually no mining activity on Bokan Mountain, the place had been abandoned. With the sudden cessation, the mining teams carelessly left behind large amounts of waste rock, mine-related equipment, and supplies. Thus, the whole mining area had twenty or more abandoned vehicles, dilapidated trailers, scores of unknown chemicals drums, and fuel tanks. All of these deleterious items produced various potential for environmental hazards to occur. Roger anticipated finding several areas of contaminated soil, tainted ground and surface waters, and air contamination in the form of poisonous radon gases likely present in the derelict underground mines.

Hunt and Brundy's scope of services were to determine the degree and extent of mine waste and other contaminates in the abandoned mine areas, the former fuel-store areas, and other equipment storage areas in the entire mining complex on the slopes of Bokan Mountain, which stands prominently at an elevation of 3,996 feet above sea level. They were also commissioned to monitor radiation levels along the mined-rock waste areas that lined the roads, along the main pathways into and out of the mined areas, and around the perimeter of other mine-claims, which were at that time, unmined.

The work also required Hunt and Brundy to sample other areas, which may have been impacted by the waste rock on Bokan Mountain. These were the claims that many geologists and engineers believed that rareearth metals were deposited in granitic intrusive bodies of rock. This area was called the *Billy Haynes III Vein*, or the *BHIII Vein*. It was named after the legendary geologist and self-made billionaire who discovered both the uranium deposits and the rare-earth vein.

Brundy was a self-proclaimed *intellectual* and avid atheist, who proclaimed that any belief in a God or Supreme Being was a total fraud. On the other hand, Hunt was a former part-time youth pastor from the Southern Baptist Convention, who held on to his deep Christian convictions; however, he had become somewhat disassociated with organized religion of late.

Roger was also known as a hard-working, serious-minded, middle-aged gentleman, but he was sometimes oversensitive to criticism and was often easily offended by others, including members of his own family, when they would find even the least of faults in his life. He had a talent to speak profoundly in public on various religious and scientific subjects. But Roger had a proclivity to get offended if he did not get the praise and accolades he felt he deserved. He claimed that if he had put so much time and effort being a volunteer youth pastor and blessing the lives of scores of young people over a period of five years at his local Bible Baptist Church in his hometown of Clovis, California, then he should have been promoted to the deacon's board or maybe even made an un-ordained assistant pastor.

Feeling deeply offended by the head pastor's comment that he was *not spiritually dedicated enough to the faith,* Roger began to slip and lag in his activity in his church, or any other church for that matter. Then about fifteen years ago, Roger totally gave up his volunteer work and focused more of his time and efforts on forming and managing his own environmental consulting firm. At that point, Roger was only a casual church attender, while his family remained active and steadfast in their church.

Roger's lack of church attendance along with his extra hours in a stressful job, caused a lot of strain on his marriage and in his relationships with his teenage children. This is when he started gambling, losing money, and being dishonest about it all. Eventually, Roger and his wife, Cindy, divorced after twenty years of marriage. About the same time, Roger decided to move his consulting company to Utah. Roger was convinced that being in the heart of the Rocky Mountains was where he needed to be in order succeed with the mining industry, which was closely related to his area of expertise. Cindy and the kids stayed in the Fresno, California area. Notwithstanding his inactivity in any particular church, Roger remained a firm defender of God and Christianity in general.

Brundy, however, never embraced any kind of religion or belief in a supreme being. Such a dichotomy of philosophical differences between the two colleagues lead to many scintillating and even heated discussions over dinner at the Dunn Hotel's restaurant, which typically consisted of delicious servings of freshly-baked salmon and other portions of seafood, including crab, halibut, and sea bass.

Brundy was not at all shy when it came to bragging about his *superior intellect* and his degree from MIT in nuclear geophysics. He was also not shy about sharing his antireligious feelings about those *crazy believers in God* and Christianity as a whole. *Religious zealots and self-righteous hypocrites,* he would call anyone who believed in any concept of a *Divine Creator.* He especially ridiculed active members of organized religion. *God did not create man, but man created God,* Brundy proclaimed a time or two. He would frequently say that *we lived in an indifferent world,* and that *if there was a God or supreme being, then why didn't he do a better job in creating a more benevolent world rather than such a world dominated by sorrow, unfairness, birth defects, and natural and manmade disasters? Why so many bad things happen that cause sadness and heartbreak*? Roger and Kurt argued and debated their views on theology every break they had, during and between their field preparations. They went at it Friday through Sunday, nearly the entire three days they were together in Ketchikan. These arguments were generally friendly in nature, and the two professionals simply agreed to disagree on their philosophical differences.

During the helicopter voyage, Roger frowned a time or two, feeling sorry for Brundy having to go through his appendectomy the night before. But he was rudely interrupted from his sympathies for his college by another series of jolts when the copter hit a new round of air turbulence. By this time, the marine waters of the Pacific Ocean around the south end of Prince of Wales Island were beginning to show their dark blue and crystalclear colors.

Roger witnessed many beautiful scenes of the coastlines of Prince of Wales Island from above in his client's favorite helicopter, which Tyler and Selos affectionately named, the *Thunder Chicken*. The flying machine got its nickname from the thunderous-crowing noise it made at take -off and its unusually slow and often jerky speed. But as quirky as the Thunder Chicken was, it never seemed to break down and with regular maintenance it worked just fine. Selos and Tylor were always joking that *it was old, but paid for in full*. Thus, it was a cheap copter cost-wise to operate for their frugal mining company.

From the sky, Roger continued enjoying the majestic blue waves slowly crashing into the jagged seashore of the remote island. No signs of sandy beaches could be seen around any of the shorelines in sight, only zagged rocks, green trees, and thick brush were seen juxtaposed against the turbid surf. From this vantage point, Roger could also see the sun rising on the horizon in the east, showing beautiful colors of pink and lavender over the mountainous mainland of the lower tip of the Alaskan panhandle. It was 0705, and they were fast approaching their destination.

Before landing at the Marina near the base camp of the former Tyler-Haynes mine area, Tyler and Selos insisted on taking GPS measurements of a few gauging stations for the several rivers and drainages running radially outward from Bokan Mountain; these measurements were part of their mapping duties as the new owners of the various mining claims. They asked Roger to take these readings by leaning out of the window of the copter while holding and reading the GPS unit. Roger was absolutely terrified to hang outside of the Thunder Chicken and take the measurements. Looking down about 500 feet below him, he could see nothing but the tops of trees, jagged rocks, and a turbulent river.

Noticing the obvious fear in Roger's eyes, Tyler said mockingly, *Come on Hunt! I thought you were a toughy*! He laughed in his typical cocky and spiteful manner. After a brief moment, Selos added a few snickers and taunts of his own. These kinds of things would usually provoke Roger to retaliate, but in the presence of his clients, he knew he had to keep his emotions to himself and let them have their fun.

Tyler was about fifty-nine years old and stood five feet six inches tall. He had a weak and frail body frame, with dark, scraggly black hair, and usually wore thick, darkframed *nerdy* glasses. He looked like one of those typical academic punks in high school or college who absolutely hated and mocked those he perceived as *jocks or athletes.*

Selos was the elder of the two geologists by about eight years, but was more of an average-sized man, standing six feet even, with wavy red hair. He was in his late-sixties and in remarkably good shape for his age. He loved showing off his muscular, freckled, Popeye the Sailor Man-like forearms. In light of how different these two clients were in their appearances and mannerisms, it was both amazing and amusing to Roger how well they got along as partners and colleagues.

Roger stood six foot-two inches tall, with a muscular body frame; he had played high school football and otherwise kept himself relatively fit throughout the last thirty-plus years through a combination of biking, hiking, backpacking, weight lifting, running, skiing, and other such fun and challenging activities. Roger was proud of his physical shape and felt good about keeping active in his middle age. But it had not always been that way throughout his life, particularly in his younger years.

In life, Roger always viewed himself as a slow starter, but a fast finisher. His sensitivities and insecurities probably developed early in life, being the youngest of four kids by about three years. He always felt like he was the typical *afterthought- child* in his family, and always regretted it. His older sister, Lisa, and his two older brothers, Davy and Freddy, were each within a year or so of each other in age, and Roger always seemed to feel left out growing up. They all went to high school together, had a plethora of common friends, and were all very popular. They were each well known as good students and talented athletes.

Roger, on the other hand, was a slow learner and reader and struggled greatly in grade school and junior high. Due to his poor grades and immaturity, he had to repeat the fourth grade. He often stuttered and mispronounced words and phrases a lot. Even though he was never formally or professionally diagnosed with the condition, Roger likely suffered from dyslexia to some degree, since he would often read and say things backwards or all mixed up. This condition would often bring on teasing and sometimes humiliation from the other kids his age, who would often verbally poke fun at him and even physically push him around from time to time. On one occasion, while in the fifth grade, Roger was ganged up on by three or four sixth graders on the playing field and was attacked, beaten, and pantsed in front of about thirty other students. With all these negative experiences, Roger had a huge chip on his shoulder, which lead to additional discouragements, more bad grades, and occasionally getting into fights with bullies at school. Roger would often find himself in detention, because everything seemed to be his fault.

Once, while in the sixth grade, a couple of Roger's friends told him that they were called in by the grade school principal and told not to hang around Roger anymore because he was the instigator of all the trouble, and they were starting to get into trouble as well. Once again, Roger's fault.

Roger's bad grades and label as a troublemaker were bad enough for his fragile selfesteem; making matters worse, was the fact that, he was also a disaster as an athlete. With every reason to be discouraged and to quit sports altogether, Roger kept trying and working hard to compete, despite his inabilities. His motivation to keep trying was due to his strong and insatiable desire to be like his brothers, whom he idolized and who excelled in just about every sport. They were always recognized by their peers and coaches as *stud athletes.*

Even his own father, Bobby Hunt, who was a star football player in high school and college in the late 1940s and early 1950s, called him his, *uncoordinated son,* and labeled him as a *slow runner* compared to his older brothers. When his own scout master once told him in a teasing manner what his father would often say about his youngest son's lack of athletic prowess, Roger was devastated and discouraged by these labels. Such experiences seemed to make life worse. All Roger wanted to do was fit in and be like his older sister and brothers, socially and physically.

Nevertheless, by the seventh grade, Roger was well on his way to failure and was labeled by classmates, teachers, and coaches as a disrupter and a problem child. All of these negative experiences resulted in a low self-esteem for Roger as he began developing many negative mind- sets, which lead to periods of depression, feelings of bitterness, and insecurities.

Despite all this, Roger somehow gradually began to develop mentally and physically. Somehow, he learned to make incremental, but steady progress in positive ways in his early to mid-teenage years. Through hard work, a growing desire to never give up, and certain individuals who influenced Roger in positive ways at critical times between the eighth and ninth grades, he began to make changes in his attitude for the better.

Also, with a few influential adults who showed a helpful interest in him, Roger found a way to overcome or saddle his deficiencies; he began to make headway in several areas. Some of these special people included a new scout master, an enthusiastic Sunday school teacher, an eighth-grade history teacher, and a football coach, who each saw potential in Roger. They also took the extra time and effort to instill elements of confidence into Roger's mind, which gave him a sense of self-determination and gradually helped him to make progress socially, spiritually, scholastically, and physically.

Roger also began reading more in high school and even took a liking to self-help books such as, *The Power of Positive Thinking*, by Norman Vincent Peale, and *How to Win Friends and Influence People*, by Dale Carnegie. By the time he was a sophomore, his grades went from Cs and Ds to mostly Bs. By his junior year, he was frequently getting As and Bs and even made the honor roll a time or two.

Roger finally made a lot of friends through church, scouts, and sports and by his senior year he also made the varsity football team as a starting defensive end. He was even named the most valuable defensive player for his team at the end of the season, which went eight wins and two losses for the year. In addition, he was also surprised and excited to be awarded All League Honorable Mention by the conference board of athletics that year. This was a huge honor for him.

He remembered, once during his senior year when the father of one of his rival teammates, Brad, who was the overall most valuable player on the team, approached him and said, *Roger, I am amazed at your progress. I'll be honest with you; I have watched you throughout the years, always struggling to be even the most mediocre of players in football and baseball. But after this year, you are the most improved player of all time in my book.* Those comments meant the world to Roger and gave him a boost in morale and confidence for years to come.

Roger went on to college, and even though he was done with team sports, he worked hard to earn a Bachelor's and Master's Degree in geology. But even with some progress and accomplishments, Roger still had his discouragements and setbacks later on in life because of his lack of faith in himself, probably stemming from the reoccurring insecurities of his youth. He was still over-sensitive, impatient, and irritable; traits which he had a difficult time overcoming.

By 0735 that Monday morning, the team had made all of the necessary GPS measurements at several locations throughout the island. Landing the Thunder Chicken in the marina at the abandoned Tyler-Haynes Mine Base Camp was next on the agenda. It would only take another twenty minutes or so to arrive at their destination. The last part of the ride was relatively smooth as the clouds burned off with the rising sun. It was becoming a beautiful, clear morning, without a cloud in the sky. *What a great start for the field expedition on Bokan Mountain,* Roger thought.

The view was beautiful and beyond description with the vivid dark blue waters of the Pacific Ocean and white frothy waves repeatedly crashing against the rocky shorelines of the south side of Prince of Wales Island. In a quiet cove or lagoon was a crescent-shaped marina, which had an old fashioned wooden dock and a tiny heliport for the Tyler-Haynes Mine base camp. Landing there was tight since the heliport was in a narrow clearing amongst the trees and brush to the side of the dock and along the rocky shoreline.

The Tyler-Haynes Mine was named after Eddie Tyler's father, Edward Tyler Sr., and Billy or William Haynes III, who were partners in a startup of the old uranium mine on Prince of Wales Island in the early 1950s. Edward had all of the corporate connections and support of Capital Mining Group, Incorporated (CMGI), the company he cofounded in the late 1940s that held all of the mining claims in and around the Bokan Mountain area on the southern tip of Prince of Wales Island.

Haynes, on the other hand, had all of the technical *know-how* in finding ore bodies, using his uncanny wits and advanced and innovative geophysical techniques that he had utilized and mastered over the years. Haynes was also adept in ore valuations and calculating the extent and volume of ore bodies. He spent many years traveling the globe on all the seven continents (including Antarctica as well), hired as a consultant and specialist by major precious metals companies such as Barrick Gold, Rio Tinto, Newmont, and countless others. He searched and found some of the largest and most lucrative ore bodies in the world, helping those companies make billions of dollars and securing the royalties. Everything Haynes touched seemed to turn into gold; as many professionals have said, Billy Haynes had the *Midas touch*.

During the summer of 1969, Edward Tyler Sr. suddenly died of a heart attack while working at the mine. There had been no way to get him to a hospital quickly enough because of his remote location, so he died in the Haynes Cabin with Billy at his bedside, within only two hours of feeling angina, pains up his left arm, then in his left shoulder, and finally, right in the center of his chest. The next thing Billy knew, Eddie was gone, leaving him the sole owner of several of the most lucrative mining deeds on Bokan Mountain.

Billy mourned for weeks after his friend's passing but steadfastly continued with the day-to -day mine operations. His mining crew was comprised of nearly one hundred professionals of various disciplines at its peak of operations in 1988—at which time Billy suddenly and mysteriously disappeared from the mine site.

Some say he was attacked and eaten by a big black bear in the northeast end of Bokan Mountain while exploring a rare-earth metal deposits. Others say he took a load of cash from the company, which went bankrupt two years later, and skipped off to a remote land in some far-off country like Monaco or somewhere along the French Riviera, living *high on the hog* the remainder of his days.

For years, Roger had been quite enamored with the legends surrounding the disappearance of Haynes as well as his storied life in general. He remembered one of the very few television interviews with the legendary William Haynes III (everyone just called him *Billy*) conducted by Barbara Walters in about 1987.

Roger remembered quite a bit from that interview, and several things actually made quite an impression on him. The most prominent thing that Roger recalled was how Billy become a self-made billionaire throughout the years, making millions upon millions of dollars from the metals and mining companies through innovation, hard work, and keen insights as a geologist and geophysicist. Then, investing well in the stock market and knowing when to buy and sell precious metals and other commodities based on market trends and other global economic changes, Billy maximized his investments. With his wealth, he also purchased thousands of acres of grazing lands in Southern Idaho to begin his second avocation, a cattle rancher for pleasure.

But what impressed Roger the most was the part of the interview when Billy made it quite clear to Ms. Walters that despite his financial successes, his greatest joy was his high school sweetheart and wife, Mary

Jane Bethers, and his three young children. He remembered how Billy's eyes welted up in tears when he described how it felt to love someone more than himself. Also during that interview, Roger was impressed to see how Billy's face glowed with pride and expressions of joy when he expressed how he strived to create a culture of Christ-centered values in their home, which included given funs and giving personal service to the abused women and children and focusing on family prayer, bible studies, and meaningful family vacations. He remembered Billy using phrases such as love and respect for all mankind, hard work, empowerment, self-determination, and goal-centered discipline and motivation for his family and business associates.

He wanted to leave a legacy for his daughter and two sons of working for *everything you get in life.* Furthermore, he wanted to be an example for his family by getting a good education, setting and achieving goals of self-mastery, and by serving others, with the crowning goal of making a positive difference in the world. According to Billy, the road to success was based on the ability to adjust your mindsets to a *healthier and more realistic way of living and avoiding negative mind-sets and their debilitating effects.* Thus, Billy's consistent theme in life was to *not focus too much on the things that you can't take with you when you die.*

Roger also remembered in sadness that part of the Walters interview focused on how Billy, at the young age of forty, tragically lost his wife, Mary Jane and three children in an auto accident on a country road about thirty minutes outside of Boise, Idaho. They were killed by a drunken driver. Upon hearing this, a sudden flash came into Roger's mind of the agony and pain Billy must have felt by losing his entire family in a single incident. Roger felt a little misty-eyed, thinking of how this horrible moment left Billy alone in life. *Since Billy was an only child, as were his late parents, he was now all alone, with no parents, no aunts or uncles, and no cousins; just him, his wealth, and his business partners,* Roger pondered in sadness.

Roger also recalled reading an article in *Forbes* magazine a few years earlier that Billy remained a bachelor, getting richer and richer, ranching from time to time in Idaho, managing mining activities in Alaska, and providing consulting services throughout the world.

Billy was never embittered by the loss of his family, but instead started travelling throughout the world more than ever before; making copious amounts of money in the precious metals industry. He became very philanthropic, quietly generously donating millions of dollars to several charitable institutions through trust funds, including organizations such as the Boy Scouts of America, March of Dimes, Red Cross, United Way, AIDS foundations and various smaller charities throughout the world.

Billy's final years were spent in the Tyler-Haynes mine on Prince of Wales Island and in the shadows and on the slopes of the majestic Bokan Mountain. The uranium mining activities were just a springboard into the finding, researching, and mining of a large vein of rare-earth metals along the northeast flanks of Bokan Mountain. Rare-earths were treasures that were little-known and not readily pursued by most mining companies until the early 1980s, after the rise of high-tech electronic and military inventions after the Cold War.

The *Forbes* article also gave some insights into Billy's progenitors and their life experiences that influenced and inspired him. William Haynes I, Billy's grandfather, was a miner in Southern Nevada in the mid-1800s and died; being poisoned at the age of forty-four, leaving a wife, Eliza, and one son, William Haynes Junior. According to both *Forbes* and folklore, William Haynes Senior held the deeds to three silver and gold mines, which ended up in the hands of his partner, who in turn sold the mine deeds to the eventual-multibillionaire, William Randolph Hearst.

Billy Junior grew up learning the ways of his father directly from a local band of Paiute Native Americans, the same people who had taught his father about finding treasures in the earth, the mysteries of nature, and the beauties of the world. Billy Junior became an amateur geologist based on Paiute wisdom and later a farmer by necessity. He was a man of high moral values, but of low financial means.

With that being considered, he made sure his son got a good education through the public school system in Las Vegas, Nevada, and worked extra hours through several part-time jobs to get Billy Haynes III into the MacKay School of Mines, now known as the Mackay School of Earth Sciences and Engineering, at the University of Nevada, Reno. Billy took it from there, earning academic scholarships and receiving bachelor and master degrees in geology and a PhD in mine engineering with an emphasis in geophysical and related technologies over the span of seven years.

Landing the Thunder Chicken at 0815 was uneventful, and as soon as the copter blades slowed their rotation enough for its crew to unload, they all piled out and conducted an orientation meeting at the Haynes Cabin, located about 250 feet up the dirt path from marina and heliport.

The meeting lasted about forty-five minutes. The log cabin at the base camp was a perfect meeting venue. It was old and rickety, and about 1,200 square feet in size: single story and no basement. With the exception of a small bathroom, the entire cabin consisted of one large room that included the kitchen, dining room, bedroom, and living area. A propane fuel tank was kept about fifty feet to the west of the cabin and was used for the kitchen stove and for heating water from a nearby well. The pantry was well stocked with a month's worth of food for at least four people. There were freeze dried meals for breakfast and dinner, and trail snacks, power bars, and water for lunch, since it was meant to be eaten in the field. The cabin was also supplied with first-aid kits for four people and a battery-operated ham radio for communication with the MMI team back at the Dunn Hotel in Ketchikan.

Tyler and Selos also provided Roger with a .44 Magnum handgun and told him to always carry it with him, if nothing else to fire off warning shots for any black bears that he may suddenly run across in the wild. If the bear wouldn't leave him alone, this caliber of gun would likely pack enough punch to sufficiently kill most adult black bears as long as he was able to aim for the head or heart—and also assuming Roger had enough time to get enough shots off and *didn't freeze up in a panic*.

Tyler and Selos instructed Roger to complete the job within eight or nine days maximum or *all hell would likely break loose* with severe weather. They hastily laid out maps and background reports of the mine areas and warned him of the hazards, man-made and natural, especially black bears.

They also joked about the possibility of seeing Billy Haynes during the next several days. Throughout the years there had been a number of alleged sightings around the old mine and Bokan Mountain by contractors, hunters, fishermen, and mining prospectors. *He was quite the old legend,* Selos said a time or two with a chuckle and a grin on his wrinkled face.

Eddie Tyler said, *If you see Uncle Billy, tell him 'hi' for me and remind him he still owes me a million bucks.*

Eddie's father and Billy were not only business partners but were as close as brothers, and Eddie had considered Billy to be an uncle figure in his life, even though he thought Billy should have left him more of the company's money in his will. The Haynes Will was still under legal dispute over the last twenty-plus years since nobody knew for sure if Billy ever died or just disappeared in some foreign land halfway around the world.

Shortly after making last-minute plans to pick up soil and surface-water samples from Roger on Wednesday, Selos and Tyler were quickly striding back to the Thunder Chicken. At 0900 sharp, the two old geologists took off and were on their way back to Ketchikan.

Roger spent rest of the day studying the maps and documents, and getting oriented around the Haynes Cabin and other nearby features, including the marina and former ore-loading and ore-storage areas, where he would need to sample soil representing residual radioactive mined waste-rock, which also would likely contain high levels of lead, arsenic, and other toxic metals, as part of an environmental hazard analyses.

Roger prepared dinner and then got an early night's rest in order to be ready for an early awaking and long day of fieldwork. He quickly feel into a deep sleep on the wood-framed twin-sized bed in the cabin and slept a good ten hours.

CHAPTER 3

A MYSTERIOUS VISITOR'S DEFINITION OF SUCCESS

Tuesday, September 26 (Expedition - Day Two):
The Silver Key Card

Roger awoke at sunrise at about 0700. To his astonishment, he noticed that there were two new items in the cabin that most certainly were not there the day before.

On the edge of the log dining table was a shiny, silver-colored rectangle-shaped object about the size of a credit card or hotel key card, but it was made of some kind of smooth metal, not plastic.

The second object was a large black castiron safe standing about four feet tall, thirty inches wide, and twenty-four inches deep, placed up against the north wall of the cabin between the kitchen and living areas. The typical-looking safe had a standard brand name, *Liberty*, written in an arch over the door, and the added label, *BHIII*, painted on the side.

For Billy Haynes III, most likely, since this was his cabin, Roger thought.

Roger thought it was strange and eerie that someone could have crept into the cabin while he was sleeping. What was even more disturbing was that this was all done without Roger being awakened or stirred in the least! He felt a chill go up and down his spine with the thought of such an invasion of his privacy.

The most unusual thing about this safe was that it had no key hole for the lock, nor did it have a combination lock—just a solid electronic-looking box with a green light and red light. The box was on the outside of the safe next to the dead bolt, which locked the door. Roger immediately deduced that the mysterious key card would open the safe and that the card had magnetic properties that signaled the safe to unlock and reveal its hidden contents.

With curiosity overruling any concern for a practical joke or a possible booby trap, Roger hastily waved the key card in front of the safe and eagerly waited for a reaction. The green light immediately lit up and the safe gave a loud clicking noise as it unlocked and slowly creaked open. As Roger shined his flashlight into the safe, he saw a metallic bust of a man's head, about eight inches in diameter, with ten blue puzzle -like pieces along each side of the bald head. Each blue puzzle piece had an acronym written on it: MST, MSE, MSA, BTW, DEW, F.A.I.R., TO-TI, PBS, NGU, and BTG. Each side of the head was a perfect mirror image of the other side. Roger picked up the bust and inspected it in amazement for a minute or two then set it down on the table, pondering its relevance.

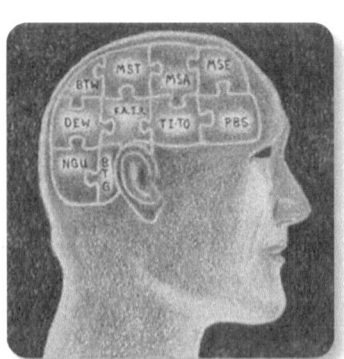

Also in the safe was a black leather folder, nine by twelve inches, with loose-leaf, hand-written pages, written in perfect cursive, totally legible; black ink on white paper. Roger quickly removed the folder and started reading the materials.

The 7 Transcending Mind-Sets of Success:
An Introduction to Mind-Set Technologies
By Billy Haynes III

Then under the title and subtitle, it read

*For Roger Hunt to read, learn, apply,
and teach to the world
This is very strange*! Roger mumbled,
*He doesn't even know me and yet he is writing this
document to me?*

Intrigued, confused, and amazed, Roger eagerly began reading the text below:

Success and Mind-Sets

Success?
Mind-sets?
What do these concepts have in common?
Everything!
Your mind-sets will determine whether you will be successful, or not. Success doesn't just happen by itself, Roger. You either make success happen—or you don't.

What is Success?

Success: A concept with a quest. A frequently-used word in our society with a multitude of personal and organizational definitions. Most would agree that the word normally is associated with surviving, thriving, achieving, and winning.

Success is something that every cognitive and proactive person strives to attain. The bottom line is this: if you are breathing and thinking, you, like most people, are probably interested in succeeding. Whether a word, a concept, an ideal, or a reality, success is arguably one of the most important and enduring things to obtain. Roger, you will first need to:

1. Define success, and then
2. Achieve success, and then
3. Sustain Success.

A miner who wants to discover and recover a precious body of ore in the earth will find it, identify it, mine it, refine it, sell it, and profit from it. In finding, mining, refining, and selling gold, the miner reaps great benefits.

Once you achieve successes in your life, you will naturally love those successes, then you will strive to live those successes and then sustain them.

Nowadays it seems that the word *success* could be considered a cliché, given the myriads of books, essays, and examples written on the subject. Everyone seems to be talking about success. Everyone wants to succeed. Everyone craves success, based on his or her own definition of the concept.

I assume here that no one really wants to fail or deliberately follows paths that lead to failure. I also assume here that everyone who wants to succeed also wants to establish worthy goals that lead to true, enduring success, and many strive throughout their lives to find what true success is.

So I ask you, Roger, the participant: what do you think true success is? How much time do you spend thinking about what true success means to you? Or should I ask: what are your mind-sets of success at this present time, and how much do those mind-sets affect the way you think and act?

What do you need to do to reach your primary goals?

A popular and worldly definition of success is creating something that sells. Variations include the following:

Amassing great **wealth**
Accumulating many physical **possessions**
Gaining **power** over others
Achieving **fame** and recognition

Is the ability to gain wealth, power, possessions, and fame the right definition of success for you? They are certainly things that many people think are important to pursue and achieve. All you have to do is read the titles of the current New York Times best sellers, view a large percentage of television ads, and witness what Hollywood exemplifies.

If obtaining wealth, power, possessions, and fame is the definition of success, then why are there so many unhappy and lost *rich and famous* people? Just read the cover to weekly *People Magazine* publication and you will see how ultimately successful the *Rich and Famous* really are.

If ultimate power and influence over others is the meaning of success, then why does this amount of ultimate power, which is imposed on others by the socialist and communist dictators, past and present, result in so much cruelty and deprivation of the most basic human rights? Why do so many of these power-hungry dictators cause so much suffering and turmoil throughout the world? These governing institutions almost always end in massive and cruel suppression, coups, wars, and ultimate failure and destruction. Was the fanciest, Adolf Hitler happy and successful? He certainly had great power and influence. He certainly aspired for ultimate power over others and had immoral and sadistic control for a period of time. But how did his life end up? How well did it work out for him in the end? How many people today revere his name?

As Paul once said, *The love of money is the root of all evil* (1 Timothy 6:10, King James Version). We can find many examples of where ultimate power corrupts ultimately. Without a doubt, all of our earthly possessions will eventually corrode, canker, and waste away.

Statistics show that most people, even these days, believe in some type of supreme being. The Pew Research Center completed a poll in April 2006 indicating that 96 percent of Americans still believe in God. Through my years of experience in working with people from around the world, I am convinced many of us believe in a God that has a great and infinite love for us, and power and supernal influence over us, either directly or indirectly. Many believers that I know from the various religious sects have faith in some type of divine and eternal rewards-and-punishments system and in the immortality of the soul of man, either spiritually or physically or both. Certainly, most people would agree that when you die, you simply cannot take your wealth, possessions, power, or positions with you into the eternities.

I believe that most logical and honest-of-heart people are capable of choosing to pursue transformational, meaningful, and personal paths to success:

- Raising a family and teaching them to live in a moral way and show love and respect for others.
- Achieving sustainable happiness and joy in one's personal life; learning to live the abundant life in the biblical sense of the word.
- Overcoming challenges and shortcomings in a path toward becoming more godlike.
- Gaining the ability to live in a provident manner; living a well-balanced life.
- Achieving the character, mental capacity, and the wherewithal to respond to and cope with each and every struggle and trial in life in a positive manner that would enable them to learn and grow from all of the good and bad things that they experience during their mortal experience.

Why this Work?

Roger, we do not need more definitions of success in this world. What we do need are better mind-sets of success—even *transcending* and magnificent mind-sets of success.

I believe and have great faith in humanity, that generally and conceptually, people are generally good and with good intentions can do incredibly wonderful things. I believe that common people are capable of solving problems in their homes and communities and are also personally capable of overcoming the challenges and trials of life in order to achieve success and become great contributors to the society and world in which we all live. But most people just do not know where and how to get started.

Unfortunately, there is only a small fraction of the nearly 6.5 billion people who currently live on earth who are willing and able to figure out a path to successful living. By nature, people do not come upon success by luck or by casually strolling upon it.

Success is not natural; it does not grow on trees, and it does not happen by itself. You have to learn and understand what success is, and then **you need to make it happen in your life** by adjusting and applying new mind-sets to your life, Roger.

Given the assumption that God did not create men and women to do nothing, you have to learn to define and achieve success by establishing goals that lead to powerful and transcending and magnificent mind-sets that will ultimately lead to an achievable framework to establish physical and spiritual wealth and influence over others in a moral and fulfilling manner. I believe that primary goals and mind-sets need to be aligned to complement each other in a way that leads people to sustainable happiness, peace, and joy—the application, experience, and enjoyment of which is true success.

With this belief, I chose to develop, cultivate, and articulate certain effective mind-sets that are in harmony with my deepest beliefs and then share these mind-sets with others so that they can help you and you can also help others. To be effective, these key mind-sets need to be the type that will transcend the common and worldly mind-sets based solely on wealth or power, which are based on greed and often become destructive and lead many people in the wrong direction.

Roger, you need to discard your destructive mind-sets as soon as possible! Destructive mind-sets include the following:

- The void or empty mind-set of idleness or the *no-mind-set syndrome*, the sore excuse of *I have no idea*. Empty and idle minds can often become filled with destructive things by default.
- Carnal minds-sets that focus on the *self* and the lustful or *natural side* of men and women that thinks it's okay to *do whatever feels good*.
- Gotta-get-rich mind-set; following the popular get-rich-quick schemes.

- Relativism theology: the belief that there is really no good or evil in the world.
- Dependency on external things: drug abuse and excessive alcohol use.
- He who has the most toys wins; keeping up with the Jones.
- Secular-only- oriented and atheistic mind-sets.
- Government dependency mind-sets.
- *I'm a victim* mind-set.
- The *arrogant intellectual* mind-sets.
- The mind-set of following latest empty fads and fashions.

Roger, I think you believe that only moral -based and transcending mind-sets will give you the confidence and positive mental attitude necessary to establish and achieve the primary and supporting goals to help you obtain true and sustainable success.

From one spiritual man to another, your primary goals, Roger, need to be in harmony with the concept that when you die, it is not the end, but only the beginning of what type of character you attain throughout the eternities. In addition to your character, it is the level of intelligence and knowledge you obtain and what you have nourished and accomplished with your closest relationships that really count from an eternal perspective.

Think of it this way and ask yourself: **What can you take with you when you die?**

The answer to this question should be easy: nothing! Nothing tangible or physical, that is. Despite their tombs and their pyramids, their hidden tunnels and their secret hiding places to stow their riches and later claim their wealth, the pharaohs of Egypt did not take their riches and treasures with them.

All we have to do is look in the museums of antiquity. Remember the time you were in Egypt, Roger? What was that, back in 1984? I have also been to Egypt.

If I recall, you were part of the university study group that was involved in the archeological excavation in the Seila-Fayum area in the western desert of Egypt during the winter of 1984, during which time you visited the Cairo Egyptian Museum. I have also visited many of the famous museums of Egypt, and I think we can both attest that King Tut's treasures are all still in those museums for us to see.

I do, however, believe that there *are* things that you can take with you when you die, things that you achieve here and can possess there in the eternities. I believe that these include

- Your individual character,
- Your knowledge and intelligence, and
- Your closest relationships.

Based on these beliefs and assumptions, Roger, shouldn't your primary and supporting goals be based upon the things that *you can* take with you when you die? Why then do we all focus so much on acquiring possessions and wealth when those things will corrode and waste away after death?

Your primary goals should also be focused on what you want to leave behind when your mortal existence is completed. Based on this thought, I would ask you, Roger, *what do you want written on your tombstone* ? How do you want to be remembered by your family, relatives, closest friends, and business associates? Your legacy is your example or your established course of goodness that you have left behind for others to follow. What would you like that to be?

Consider the Two Tombstones analogy.

The Two Tombstones Analogy

What do you want written on your tombstone Roger? Your Mind-set Adjustment takes place when you create the vision of what you want to achieve by the time you reach the twilight of your life.

The Two Tombstones analogy gives an example of two extremes: The Jean Begone (pronounced, *Bee-goown*) Tombstone and the Sam Invest Tombstone as shown below:

Jean Begone

Here lies the pretentious Jean Begone.
He worked his fingers to the bone.
His only goal was to earn great wealth.
He did not consider good wisdom or health.
His road to success was clouded by greed.
He lost his family and his friends indeed.
He had no value-directions or goals.
He had no vision, he paid great tolls.
He made no time for family or God.
He lost his soul for money and fraud.
And when he was gone and he was dead,
And when all was done and all was said,
The pretentious Jean Begone
Without victory, was left alone.

Contrast Jean Begone with Sam Invest:

Sam Invest

Here lies the honorable Sam Invest.
The life he lived was a great success.
He had great vision, he experienced great health.
His talents he grew, he too had some wealth.
But he balanced his time for family and friend
And with much service, great blessings, no end.
He imparted his talents to those in need.
He learned great lessons and had no greed.
He will always be loved by those he served.
He was labeled great husband, beloved father.
Forever and ever he was the truest friend.
He was his best to the very end.
He was devoted and honest, he was loyal and true.
He would always be there, you always just knew.
When he left this life he took all this,
His character and relations with eternal bliss.

It is your recipe for success and your entryway onto the pathway of success, which actually begins with the last chapter of your life, the conclusion, the epilogue.

This is your plan; therefore, you create your own ending; now, based on what you feel is most important for you and for those you are leaving behind.

All of this emphasis is important because the only thing in life that is 100 percent certain is your death; sooner or later you will die. Therefore, plan now for how you would like those closest to you (your family, relatives, friends, and associates) to remember you.

In the blank tombstone provided below, Roger, write what you would desire those closest to you to say about you when you have finally left them. Outline below what you want written in your last chapter in life on your tombstone.

(Write how you want to be remembered in the spaces below.)

Name:_____

What do you want written on your tombstone by the people you leave behind?

You should begin your goal-setting journey fortified with the transcending mind-sets that you believe in and that will help you toward what you have defined as true or lasting success. And because these mind-sets are transcending the destructive, the useless, and the common mind-sets of the dark end of the world, these become magnificent; magnificent, because they will be morally and biblical-based and they will have both purpose and perspective and lead to magnificent results in lasting joy and happiness. One common definition of the adjective magnificent that is found in written works might read: Works and achievements that are very good, impressive, beautiful, elaborate, extravagant, and even *striking*. The origin of the word is from late-middle English via Old French from Latin, meaning: *making great* based on *Magnus great*.

As you are able to define success and map out a personal plan to achieve success-oriented goals, there may be a few additional thought-provoking questions you may wish to consider to ensure that you are committed to succeeding.

Roger, continue reading **only** if you were able to answer *yes* to the questions below. So I ask you: are you willing to:

- Continue to trod the path and endure the many setbacks that often thwart your progress along the way to success?
- Endure the pain that leads to the gain?
- Sustain the gain with long-term commitments to the basic and transcending principles that lead to sustainable success?
- Hang in there and go all the way with your goals to sustain your success and even learn to help others in the process?
- Are you ready to let magnificence happen in your live?

Okay, Roger, now that **you are willing** to commit to the road that leads to sustainable success, there is one other important aspect of success that is important to consider:

Successful achievement of good things is not finite or limited to any particular person, to any certain people or class of people. There are no empty cupboards in this world in terms of enough real opportunities for any honest-of-heart seeker of success.

People can't honestly say that because their neighbor or their rival has been successful with temporal or enduring achievements that they should be envious of those achievements. **Success is abounding**.

There is an abundant field of blessings to go around for all proactive and self-determined souls.

Success, is inherently:

- **Abundant:** Other people's successes do not limit your ability to succeed, nor do your successes limit the ability for others to succeed. Success and the rewards of success are plentiful and there are a plethora of opportunities that can abound for all who will follow the path that leads to success.
- **Enduring:** If you will endure the challenging experiences while striving for success and be patience with yourself and the timing of achieving ever increasing and inevitable results, the rewards of success will help you endure the difficult road forward.
- **Timeless:** The principles of success apply to all ages and do not change or become antiquated. You also should never make the mistake to think that because you have not succeeded yesterday or today that you cannot succeed tomorrow.
- **Infinite:** The rewards of success will never be minimized or limited to the effects of worldly influences.
- **Sustainable:** Staying on the path of success will lead to selfperpetuating actions that will spontaneously produce results that in turn will nurture and bless you and those around you with rich rewards.
- **Universal:** The principles of success and the path that leads to success apply to all and are not dependent upon age, gender, race, or national origin.

Failure is not permanent unless you fail to improve and overcome setbacks by making adjustments to your ineffective ways of thinking and destructive mind-sets. On the other hand, success can be both **magnificent and permanent** if you continuously strive to maintain it and sustain it the way you have obtained it.

These writings are about your pathway to success, Roger; I wrote these concepts for you, because these words of wisdom are all about you, or at least they can be about you. Roger, you should apply these concepts and the many to follow, to your own life. You will find that as you learn and adopt improved mind-sets, practice them, and write about them, that you will not only be able to overcome your addiction to gambling, but you will also be able to help others as you move forward in your life.

You need better tools, Roger. You also need a divine and eternal perspective to move forward. Roger, I know, and I perceive that you too believe that there is a God in the highest of heavens who wants to bless and help you. But, only if you want His help and reach out to Him, will He in turn give you the humility, strength, and divine perspective you need to move forward. Roger, think of it this way: This could be the beginning of writing your own book on how to save yourself and help others along the way as well.

Roger, I offer you a challenge and a promise: I challenge you: to learn, apply, adopt, and live the magnificent and transcending mind-sets of success, which I am about to present to you while you are here along on this island. Thus, I challenge you to become a Magnificent Mind-set Man in your own right and teach others these wonderful concepts by example and experience.

As you are able to do this Roger, I promise you that you will not only be able to overcome your addictions, self-doubt, anger, and mediocrity; but, you will also be enlightened and divinely directed to express and write about your successes. You will be able to expound to others how you overcame your negativities in your own words and through your own experiences. You will soon see that as you become a Magnificent Mind-set Man, that it will be natural to seek out and help others learn and adopt transcending mind-sets and learn of the joy in the whole process. This pathway forward leads to becoming the kind of person you really want to be.

CHAPTER 4

A TIMELY INTRODUCTION

It took Roger about twenty minutes to read and ponder Billy's writings. It took another thirty-five minutes to get dressed and prepare his freeze-dried eggs-and-sausage breakfast, which was surprisingly, hot, tasty, and very satisfying. During this time of field preparation, Roger couldn't help being blown away mentally and emotionally with the idea that a stranger from the past, whom he has never met, could know all about him in so many ways; this stranger knew all about his gambling addiction, his strengths and weaknesses and what he really needed to do in his life. Despite all this and his concern that someone had covertly entered the cabin the night before, Roger was intrigued with these personal and inspiring writings and couldn't wait to read more; but at the moment, he was out of pages and out of time.

Roger knew he needed to start collecting soil and surface-water samples and work on his other field duties planned for the day. Since it was almost 0800, he wanted to stay on schedule with a busy day of work ahead of him.

Roger left the Haynes Cabin all packed with field supplies, site maps, lunch, sample containers (8-ounce glass jars), and, of course, his fully loaded .44 Magnum for protection.

Not far down the path from the cabin, toward the marina sampling location, Roger heard a sudden scream of a bald eagle. The sound echoed throughout the marina. It was a startling and majestic call, and it pierced Roger's mind and heart. It was followed by a profound silence throughout the marina. As Roger turned toward the source of the cry, he spotted the noble and magnificent creature gracefully soaring over the marina, as if the eagle was eager to pronounce his blessing upon a newfound visitor at the dawn of a beautiful and crisp day on the slopes of Bokan Mountain.

This was Roger's first intimate experience with a bald eagle in the wild. Despite his many travels and adventures throughout the past twenty years, this was an awesome and unique experience for Roger, and it seemed to be a wake-up call to him personally. This *call of the wild* seemed to prompt Roger's mind to recall all of what he had read just minutes ago. The call also seemed to endow him with a hypnotic ability to memorize and recall the writings in the *BHIII Memoir*. Within seconds, Roger was overwhelmed with a mental and intellectual boost, a feeling of optimism, and a newfound sense of selfdetermination, desiring more than ever before to follow a path toward a more successful and happy life. In an instant, Roger recalled every word of the BHIII writings, and he knew of their importance to him personally as well as those he loved.

After a few short moments of pondering and self-reflection, Roger came to himself and momentarily set aside this experience to resume his work without further delay. He immediately headed toward the ore staging and loading areas in the marina portion of the mining complex. These used to be the primary areas used to store and systematically stage the uranium ore before loading it onto barges; from there, the ore was shipped to ports in Seattle and then further transported by rail to the Rocky Mountains for processing at mills in Utah and Colorado.

Roger noted that these areas were roped off and had standard yellow radiation signs to warn workers and visitors of the mining complex. Another warning sign read, *Use extreme caution in these areas and do not spend more than two hours per year at these locations!*

No kidding! Roger thought sarcastically as he hastily got into and out of the hazardous sampling areas as quickly as he could. He hoped that as long as he did not linger any longer than the time required to collect his surface-soil samples, he would be safe without needing to don a specialized radiation suit. Instead, rubber gloves, protective eyewear, and standard cleanup materials would be sufficient to protect him for these short-term exposures to the residual radiation that may still be present in soil in those areas.

Roger completed these activities in less than twenty minutes and then labeled and secured the samples in laboratory glass jars in coolers, which were then stored in the Haynes Cabin. The samples were to be picked up by Tyler and Selos the next day, sometime in the afternoon.

Then, up the path to the west, Roger headed to the abandoned mining operations along the southern slopes of Bokan Mountain. As Roger briskly walked up the dirt road leading to the underground uranium mines, he noted various dilapidated mining-related supplies, equipment, vehicles, and trailers littering the sides of the roads, which were largely overgrown by the vegetation.

Within a mile up the path was a fork in the road. Roger saw more signs warning of hazards and radiation exposure pointing to the left: *Underground Mines, 0.9 miles.* Another sign, which pointed to the right, read, *Open-pit Mines 2.5 miles and Precipice Lake 7.9 miles.* Roger's job for the day was to evaluate environmental hazards and collect soil and stream water samples in the areas around the underground mines.

Taking the path to the left, Roger soon observed that the road was becoming more and more narrow and less defined as the forest seemed to swallow up the more obvious remnants of the old mining activities. During the next half-mile or so, the signs of mining reappeared, and suddenly many abandoned structures, vehicles, rusted conveyors belts, and miscellaneous debris reappeared into an ugly collage resembling an abandoned junk yard. Roger saw potential areas of hazardous waste, including oil spills and spills of other petroleum-related chemicals from corroded aboveground storage tanks and rusted fifty-five gallon metal drums. Areas of contamination were found just about everywhere for the next 1,000 feet along the narrow road. Roger spent the next two hours photographing the surrounding area and sampling locations, documenting the hazards, and sampling soil around each of the contaminated areas.

Then at the end of the road Roger saw a mine adit (mine opening) and, as it came into full view, a stream flowing out of the man-made cavern. According to the field map, this stream was named Miner's Creek; it started from the mine opening and flowed out along the southern slopes of Bokan Mountain at the south end of Prince of Wales Island and slowly made its way to the Pacific Ocean.

Roger remembered that his environmental assessment scopes of work included sampling any surface water that may have come into contact with any mine waste rock, fuel-storage areas, or other chemical contamination. It was obvious to him that any water emanating from this mine would most certainly have been impacted by residual radiation from the uranium rock. Therefore, Roger spent the next thirty minutes collecting surface water samples from Miner's Creek.

At the end of sampling, Roger was strongly tempted to enter into the underground mine. He thought if he could find some worthwhile, pocket-sized tools, coins, or other cool mining artifacts, that would really make his day.

The mine opening was round, about seven to eight feet in diameter as it entered into the side of steep cliff. The area around the mine adit was covered by dense forest overgrowth, loose rock, and waste rock scattered about. The adit was not easily found unless one was standing directly in front of it, looking straight at the opening.

As Roger entered, he immediately felt the discomfort of walking on the jagged rocks, which were randomly lying on the floor of the mine. Then a few feet farther inward, Roger felt a damp mist on his face emanating from several shallow pools of water near the mine's opening, which were the probable headwaters of Miner's Creek. Roger also immediately experienced an unpleasant musty odor as he continued a litter deeper into the mine, which he speculated was a combination of mold and animal waste. Being distracted by these dank and foul odors, Roger soon found that he was stumbling over dozens of tube-shaped rock cores, each about two inches in diameter and three to five feet in length. The cores were likely part of the former mineral exploration phases of past mining activities. Roger concluded that these relics were strewn about inside the mine as the last crew of the miners hastily unloaded them into the underground mine, probably when the mining activities suddenly ceased in the late-1980s.

As he continued in about thirty to forty feet, the cave made a gradual turn to the right, and then things got darker and darker and colder and colder. With his flashlight and the minimal amount of light still available from the mine opening, Roger's eyes suddenly focused on something that looked like bones lying scattered on the rocky floor in a dry area of the mine. At first, this brought a sense of fear, thinking they could be from a human, but upon further scrutiny he concluded that they were more likely from an animal, probably a deer that had fallen prey to a hungry bear preparing for winter hibernation.

Distracted by the bones and the thought of bears in the cave, Roger was suddenly spooked by the fluttering and high-pitch squeaking of scores of cave bats flying within inches of his head and out toward the cave entrance. The thought of bats flying that close to him sent chills up and down Roger's spine. That scare along with the bones, nearly convinced him to turn around and flee the mine at that moment. However, his overwhelming curiosity about what treasures could be discovered ahead encouraged him to continue on further.

As Roger continued in another thirty, forty, and then fifty paces, the cave seemed to be getting colder, darker and more damp. Soon, Roger felt like he was swallowed up in almost total darkness. Even the light of his average- sized flashlight could barely penetrate the abyss. Only a glimmer of light could been seen in the direction of the mine opening from whence he came. Also, since Roger brought no coat, he began to shiver intermittently as the increasing cold and dampness of the mine penetrated every square-inch of his body.

At this point, the cave opened up into a large, early circular room. Roger began looking around the large open area of the cave; flashing his light to the right, he began walking in that direction. Then he discovered a steep-sided pool of dark water near the center of the room. It looked very deep with the minimal light from Roger's dim flashlight. It also appeared that this pool fed the water in the cave floor and was a likely source of Miner's Creek. The nearly black waters and bottomless depth of this pool seemed to mesmerize Roger, drawing him near the water's edge. As Roger stepped closer and closer toward the rocky edge, he slowly leaned over and peered into the mysterious aqueous cauldron below him. With a faint mist floating on the surface of the black water, he shinned his light to probe for a bottom or broad ledge that may be perching trove of treasure or other valuable artifacts. But seeing no bottom or treasure, only darkness, Roger began to feel his equilibrium compromised and he also became unsure of his footing. Fear began to replace curiosity. Sensing the danger, Roger slowly began backing away from the hazard, realizing that his carelessness could have easily led to possibly stumbling and falling into this watery pit. He thought of how foolish he just was. *I could have slipped, bumped my head, and fallen in unconsciously. I would have never been heard from again. How stupid of me.*

With this sudden realization, Roger began seeing mental images of his dear wife Julie with her beautiful smile, pearly white teeth, thick and lush brunette hair, and deep brown eyes. He just wanted to be safe and return to her in one piece and feel her arms around him again. He also had flashes of each of his four children Ricky, Michael, Allyson, and Valerie. They were each young adults pushing marriage and having children. He wanted to ensure that he would stay alive long enough to be a grandfather, so he continued slowly and surely backing away from the pool until he felt safe again.

In retreat from the pool, Roger began shining his dim light along the walls and ceilings of the cave room and noticed that many of the granitic rocks were magically stained with a deep red-blood type of iron-oxide or more specifically, hematite bodies and streaks running in every direction throughout the parent rock. Roger remembered that, according to the reports he read concerning the uranium ore, this type of staining was indicative of the highest grade of uranium ore on Bokan Mountain.

This must be the mother lode of uranium, Roger thought. *Maybe this is where they stopped mining when the Cold War came to an end and uranium mining at the Tyler-Haynes Mine became unsustainable.*

To his left, Roger suddenly noticed an old wooden box labeled *TNT*. Cautiously approaching the box, he opened the lid, and fearfully observed that it was partially filled with sticks of dynamite. Speculating that this decaying supply of explosives could be unstable, he gladly left it alone and began walking toward the main arterial path that led back to the entrance. But in doing so, Roger nearly tripped over a small curious-looking antique light brown colored stone chest or box about twelve inches long, eight inches wide, and eight inches tall. The object was sitting on a short flat rock as if the owner had recently placed it there for someone like him to easily find. This type of artifact was exactly the kind of treasure Roger was hoping to find and possibly collect.

The minimal light from his flashlight revealed that this little chest was made of pure Egyptian alabaster, very similar to other similar artifacts he had seen in Egyptian museums in Cairo more than twenty years ago during his graduate studies in that part of the world. It looked ancient in nature and ornate in design, with Egyptian-like hieroglyphics on each of the four sides and lid. Roger guessed its weight at about eight to ten pounds.

He could not wait to open the chest and see if he had just won an archaeological lottery. Based on its relatively light weight, Roger did not expect to find any large amounts of gold, silver, or any other precious metals. Upon giving the chest a little shake, he was, though a little exited to hear what he thought was the sound of a metallic rattle of something with potential significance or value. Roger was puzzled to see there was no apparent depression or latch to open the chest, reminding him of the safe back at the cabin. And since he was anxious to open the chest without breaking it open, he remembered that he had put the silver card key in his right front pocket before leaving the cabin.

Maybe, just maybe, this card will also open the chest, like it did the safe at the Haynes Cabin, he thought.

Pulling the card out of his pocket, he quickly waved it in front of the alabaster chest, and the top lid cracked open. But much to Roger's chagrin, the contents that spilled out onto the cave floor consisted of eight new metallic cards, each just like the silver card he was holding in his hand. Each of the new cards was a specific color; one was gold and the rest were the seven colors of the rainbow: violet, indigo, blue, green, yellow, orange, and red.

Roger put each of the nine key cards, including the silver card, back into the alabaster chest and then took out the gold card by itself and shined his flashlight on its smooth, shiny surface.

To Roger's surprise, he soon found that depending on the angle of the light and the card with respect to each other, he could create a three-dimensional holographic image that illuminated itself against the smooth cave wall. The image that appeared was that of the head identical to the one that he found in the safe that morning and held in his hands. It was a vivid and three-dimensional image of a bald man's head with the same shape, colors, metallic appearance, and puzzle pieces as on the tangible figurine that he had left back in the cabin that morning. Rather than remaining a static illumination, it eerily seemed to be in motion, slightly and slowly moving or pivoting from side to side. Roger immediately thought about the real figurine back at the Haynes Cabin and messages he had read from the writings he found in the safe that morning and spontaneously thought to name the figurine and the image before him *The Mind-Set Man*. And because this image was so wonderful and amazing, Roger felt that a better name for this figurine would be the *Magnificent Mind-set Man*.

Roger sensed that the *Magnificent Mind-Set Man* was telepathically speaking to him in a way that he could not describe, but he knew that the image was trying to communicate something important. The thoughts that came into his mind simply said, *Roger, learn to evaluate your mind-sets and adjust your thinking and actions to coincide with The 7 Transcending Mind-Sets of Success.*

That message was repeated three times. After the third time, the acronyms MST, MSE, and MSA flashed brightly on each side of the Mind-Set Man's head, which was noticeable as the figurine pivoted from side to side, and then continued to be illuminated on the wall. The puzzle pieces suddenly turned gold as they stopped flashing.

Roger immediately speculated that the combination of the light on the card, which was probably composed of a combination of highly conductive and magnetic rare earth metals, and the angle he held the light relative to the card, which reflected against the radioactive minerals in the rocks of the cave room, was the mechanism that mysteriously, but scientifically created the image.

Even though Roger put the gold card back into the chest and pulled out another card, the Magnificent Mind-Set Man image remained on the wall for the next several seconds. He then held up the violet card and positioned it with the light in the same manner and angle as with the gold card.

To his astonishment, Roger witnessed a completely different illumination appearing to the right of the Magnificent Mind-Set Man. This new image was of two large, glowing, pale hands gently holding an infant, in a manner that Roger interpreted as a new child being delivered to the world and to her mother by the gentle and commanding hands of the loving God.

The Magnificent Mind-Set Man image again communicated in the same uncanny way as before: *Roger, you and all mankind were* born to win!

As this message was repeated three times, the BTW acronym (meaning Born to Win) began to flash on another puzzle piece, which continued for several seconds, until it stopped flashing and turned violet.

As he continued through the remaining six cards in the same manner, a new figure and message appeared against the wall to the right of the one before it in a sequence.

The indigo card illuminated an image of a red apple with a brownish stem. There were bites taken out of the apple on each side and the Mind-Set Man's telepathic message was *Defeat entropy and win*, repeated three times, and the acronym DEW was illuminated on another puzzle piece on the Magnificent Mind-Set Man, which turned indigo.

The blue card illuminated an image of a magnifying glass with the word *F.A.I.R* imprinted in the center of the lens. The message was: *Learn the F.A.I.R principals to goal setting*, repeated three times, and the acronym F.A.I.R. was illuminated on another puzzle piece on the Magnificent Mind-Set Man, which turned blue.

The green card illuminated an image of a green disc, and in the center were the phrases *Turned-in* and *Turned-out*, with arrows pointing into and out of the central disc. The message was: *Learn to be turned-out and win*, repeated three times. The acronym TI-TO was then illuminated on another puzzle piece on the Magnificent Mind-Set Man, which turned green.

The yellow card illuminated an image of a man walking, a cloud, and a bolt of lightning coming from the cloud immediately above the man's head. The Magnificent Mind-Set Man telepathically communicated the phrase *Peace, be still*, repeated three times, and *How is your personal weather forecast?* That message was also repeated three times. The acronym PBS then appeared on another puzzle piece on the Magnificent Mind-Set Man, which turned yellow.

The orange card illuminated an image of ski poles, a soccer ball, a baseball bat and ball, and a black belt from Karate. The Magnificent Mind-Set Man said, *Never give up*, repeated three times. The acronym NGU then appeared on another puzzle piece on the Magnificent Mind-Set Man, which turned orange.

The red card illuminated an image of two perpendicular lines, a vertical y-axis and a horizontal x-axis, geometrically forming a right angle, with seven steps leading upward from right to left right in a stair-like manner inside the x- and y-axes. The Magnificent Mind-Set Man said, *Grow from base to grace, BTG, and learn the Seven Divine Characteristics for Permanent Success*. The acronym BTG then appeared on another puzzle piece on the Magnificent Mind-Set Man, which turned red.

Roger gasped and steadied himself when he saw all eight images suddenly disappear, and the cave room was dark again with only his dim flashlight. This unprecedented visual display from the metallic cards, the illumination of Roger's dim flashlight, and this strange and Magnificent Mind-set Man, penetrated deeply into Roger's mind and heart as he began pondering the meaning of this moment.

During the next 30 seconds, Roger stood nearly paralyzed with a bewildered look on his face. As Roger continued to stand in silence and amazement, continuing to ponder the significance of his electronic vision during the next 30 seconds, his expressions of amazement morphed into feelings of reverence for this almost, sacred moment. Then, the feeling of reverence was suddenly replaced with feelings of greed and pride. The cave got darker and colder than before as Roger began thinking less than reverent and spiritual thoughts. As the feelings of greed and pride got stronger and stronger, Roger's began saying words like, *I will study these precious items, figure out the science related to the mysteries of these metallic cards, and make millions of dollars with this technology and information*. At that moment, Roger's flashlight began to flicker and fade.

As Roger's light continued to diminish over the next few seconds, he soon began to fear for his safety since he was alone in the darkness with minimal light with many potential unknown hazards around him. The constant drip of water from the cave ceiling and the continuous trickle of water running along the floor of the cave floor seemed to mesmerize and then frighten him. The musty-damp smell of mine also added to his discomfort.

Oh No! Roger's foot suddenly slipped on a damp rock. With his teeth clinched, he lost his fragile balance and he fell backwards on the rocky cave floor. He was relieved to find that he had fallen on his backpack, which cushioned the impact. The good news was that he did not sustain any injuries except a scuffed-up elbow, a slightly sprained wrist, and shattered pride. The bad news was that his flashlight must have been damaged since there was no sign of light at all in the cave; everything was completely dark. Roger fumbled around on the ground for a few minutes and finally found his flashlight. With a little effort, he was able to get it turned on after a moment of flicking the switch and shaking it around; however, the light was very dim at this point and it wasn't much help in the dark.

During the fall, Roger also dropped the alabaster chest and lost everything, including the cards into the dark and the interstitial gaps in the rocks on the cave floor. Then suddenly, there was one faint glimmer seen with his dim light over to his left. It was only one of the nine key cards: the gold one, which he quickly secured in his left pant pocket.

As Roger stood back up on this feet, he froze in his tracks as he began to panic, fearing the many dangers that he had carelessly and unwittingly stumbled across. He thought about how easy it would be to misstep into the pool or another deep hole that he hadn't seen before.

He thought of all the loose rocks of the cave floor and along the sides of an unstable mine. *Could wall rocks be loosened by grabbing onto one or by bumping into the wall causing a cave-in? I could be crushed to death.* He thought again of Julie and his children feared how he might never see them again if his luck did not soon change.

Roger also remembered that during his preparation for this expedition he read about the hazards of radon gases that typically build up in the underground workings at the Tyler-Haynes mines and how these gases could reach up to a thousand times greater than what the U.S. Environmental Protection Agency (EPA) would consider safe for breathing conditions. He offered a quick but sincere prayer in his heart to his Heavenly Father for comfort and deliverance from this potentially treacherous moment.

Then, immediately, Roger heard a stern but whispering-like voice that warned him against staying in the mine any longer. The voice comforted and assured him that if he started out immediately and followed the light of the mine entrance that he would be safe. Within a second or two, Roger regained the confidence he needed and quickly obeyed the voice. He also noticed that the light around the corner toward the entrance of the mine was noticeably lighter than just a moment ago, which further added to his confidence. Shining the dim light to the ground to ensure good footing, he continued following the light from the mine opening as it gradually got lighter and lighter towards the opening. Soon Roger felt completely safe again as he exited the mine. He was chagrined by the loss of the chest and all but one of the key cards, but was just glad to be safely out of the underground mine.

With haste, Roger gathered up all his gear and samples and headed back up the path to the Haynes Cabin. He realized that the whispering voice, which he heard and obeyed was both a comfort and a confidence-booster to him when he needed it the most. The reassuring words from an angel or mysterious guide was what he needed at that very moment to avoid a total panic, which may have led to making a rash decision, or dangerous move. He also recognized that the help he received, had likely saved his life. Roger was humble and grateful to his Lord for that moment of deliverance from great danger.

As he continued back to the Haynes Cabin, he pondered this whole experience and was confused about the origin of the whispering voice. *Was it an audible voice from a person hiding in the dark?* Roger thought. *Or was it a spiritual prompting from guiding spirit-entity that I heard in my mind or that miraculously entered into my heart in answer to a desperate and sincere prayer?*

Regardless, Roger felt grateful and blessed that he was safe again and back on his way to completing his goals for the expedition. He realized that any injury would have been bad: at best, a minor injury could have delayed completing his job, at great expense to his company and his clients' company; and at worst, his carelessness could have led to a severe injury or his death.

Back at the cabin at 1535, Roger finished labeling and packing up his samples that he had collected earlier that day at the underground mine area. He knew he needed to be ready for Tyler and Selos to pick these samples up the following day. He looked over his maps and reread the investigation's work plan to consider if he had missed any sampling areas that he could still complete before night fall. While perusing the work plan and the site map, Roger identified one area that he should have sampled: the mine's backup generator site, which, according to the reports, had an aboveground oil tank that was leaking. The ground around the old tank needed to be sampled for diesel fuel contamination.

By this time, it was approaching 1605, but Roger wanted to sample that area before sundown to get all of the sampling done the day before the sample pickup. This plan would keep him ahead of schedule, which would impress his clients considering this work was originally planned to be a two-person job.

The generator site was located approximately halfway up the road from the Haynes Cabin and the fork leading to the underground -mine area where Roger spent the most of the morning and early afternoon. The generator area was off the mining road by a hundred yards or more, uphill, in a forested area, and in a small clearing. Thus, it would be a little difficult to find, to say the least. But Roger felt confident that if he followed the map closely to a certain sign that should be posted on a tree along the way, he should be able to find the location where he would have to leave the mine road and find the generator site. He knew if his plan was followed closely he could realistically collect the needed soils samples and be back to the cabin by dusk.

He was looking forward to have a relaxing dinner of freeze-dried stew that night. He also pictured in his mind that he could make a cozy fire in the cabin's fireplace and have a wonderful rest that evening pondering his visionary experience in the underground mind and the written principles of success that he had learned earlier that morning from Billy's writings. Also, remembering the call of the wild that he had experienced as he left the cabin that morning, Roger felt assured that he could use and build upon those fascinating words that he had learned. The events of the day caused Roger to start feeling that there was a greater purpose to him being on Prince of Wales Island than just the expedition he was completing for his clients. He felt blessed being inspired by the eagle's call and protected by the whispering voice in the underground mine.

But little did Roger know how true those feelings were and how personal he would get with the BHIII writings until the events over the next hour played out. Roger's feelings of comfort and confidence would soon be tested to the extreme.

Following the map with exactness, Roger left the mining road at the point where a rusted signpost on a tree read, *Generator Site 500 Feet West*, with an arrow pointing the way ahead to the site of the last sampling location of the day. Roger found the clearing and the generator site with little trouble and was able to sample the contaminated soil in three locations without incident.

After carefully placing the glass sample containers into his pack, he started on his way back to the mining road. But he soon found that he was heading in a different direction; either slightly or greatly he did not know. He suddenly did not remember seeing the same trees, rocks, and brush as he did on his way to the generator site.

He wisely began retracing his footsteps back to the generator site, thinking he could get back there safely and then find the right way back to the mining road. As he turned to his head slightly to the left, to his amazement and horror, he spotted an adult black bear with her two cubs about 100 to 125 feet ahead in a meadow-like clearing.

As Roger froze, still as a statue and quiet as a cat, he noted that she was aggressively digging into a fallen and decaying Douglas Fir tree, probably hungrily feeding upon tree beetles, grubs, or some other insects. While one cub was trying to do the same as mother, the other had playfully wandered away and was about one-third of the way along a line directly between Roger and the mother bear.

As cute and innocent as this seemed, Roger immediately knew he was in grave danger. Without panicking, he began thinking logically. *Which way is the wind blowing? Am I up wind from the bear or downwind? Downwind would be better so she wouldn't catch my scent.*

Maybe if he could turn and sprint away, he would go unnoticed and escape the pending danger. If he only knew where and how far away the main mining road was. Then he thought of the .44 Magnum handgun in his pack. *Could I take my pack off fast enough to arm myself and either scare her off, or shoot and kill her in self-defense if she started charging?* All these thoughts seemed to come into his mind within a millisecond of time.

Then suddenly, Roger sensed that same piercing and whispering voice he heard in the mine earlier that afternoon, which said, *Don't shoot the bear, Roger. Just run to the road now and get to the cabin as quickly as you can! Don't look back.*

Roger heard the voice but did not immediately obey the advice. Instead, he remained planted in his frozen and fearful state. The bear, either by hearing or smelling something, looked straight up in Roger's direction. She then stood on her hind legs momentarily and let out an angry and frightening roar that Roger would never forget. As if in slow motion, she started charging on all fours at Roger, who remained frozen in his tracks. With a surge in adrenaline, Roger reached into his pack, grabbed his gun, removed the safety, and pointed the weapon with trembling hands at the charging mother bear.

At this instant, an old man jumped from nowhere directly in front of Roger's gun. Yelling at the top of his lungs the old man said, *Don't shoot, I said! Just run straight to your left—you'll find the road. Get to the cabin! I'll take care of Chloe.*

Roger immediately obeyed the welcomed intruder, and with the gun still in his hand, he sprinted straight toward the old mining road, took a quick left, and continued running until he reached the Haynes Cabin. Out of breath and in haste, Roger quickly opened the door and slammed it shut behind him. He immediately locked it from the inside. He put the gun down on the table and took his pack off. He was still trembling and was breathing rapidly, nearly to the point of hyperventilating. He was also scared witless. But also soon felt the great sense of relief to be safe.

I'm safe, he sighed.

But who was this stranger? Roger wondered. *How did he arrive at that critical time? Did he escape the charging bear or was he attacked? He called her Chloe, as if he knew this bear, as if it were some kind of pet that he had trained or had some mysterious powers over.* All these thoughts and questions stormed into Roger's mind as he was still catching his breath.

Could this have been the legendary Billy Haynes? Or just a brave wanderer who fortuitously found and miraculously saved me? Could it be true that that Billy Haynes was still alive and was still wandering about the Tyler-Haynes Mine, or was he a ghost that protected or haunted the area?

Roger only got a quick glimpse of the old-timer, but the image of his face was permanently burned into his mind. He compared the memory with a framed picture on the fireplace mantle showing Billy Haynes standing alongside the late Edward Tyler Sr. The man in the photo was the same person Roger had met just moments ago, he was sure. Only the man whom he had abruptly met that day looked a little older and considerably hairier.

The other thing that Roger knew for sure was that he was safe, and he was grateful for that. He immediately kneeled and prayed to his Lord with a thankful and humble heart for deliverance.

As Roger rose from his humbled posture, he immediately remembered that he still possessed the gold key card, which he had firmly placed into his left pocket while still in the underground mine.

Without hesitating, he eagerly waved it at the safe. Again it readily opened. Inside were the same figurine of a man's head and the same leather folder, but with additional pages.

Roger began reading the additional text, under the title *Mind-Set Technologies*.

CHAPTER 5

A BETTER PATH: MIND-SET TECHNOLOGIES

Tuesday, September 26 (Expedition - Day 2 [contd]): The Gold Key Card

Roger began reading the following:

Mind-Set Technologies: Transcending from the Ordinary to the Magnificent.

Roger, with the assumption that most everyone wants to be more successful in life, you need to help others develop the most effective and transcending mind-sets that will help them obtain enduring and meaningful success. Learn to transcend from the ordinary, the common, the ineffective mind-sets, to magnificent mind-sets.

Mind-Set Technologies is a unique and transformative process designed to help ordinary people accomplish great and magnificent things and create a happier, more successful way of life for themselves and those around them.

Establishing and focusing on success-oriented goals is the pathway to experiencing a more fulfilling life. Establishing worthy goals is one thing, but achieving those goals is another. This is where *Mind-Set Technologies* comes in.

Mind-Set Technologies (MSTs) is a two- step process that can easily be learned and effectively applied. The first step in Mind-Set Technologies is known as the Mind-Set Evaluation (MSE), which is designed to help you honestly examine your current habits (good or bad) and your current ways of thinking and living (thus, your current mind-sets), and evaluate whether or not those habits and mind-sets are conducive to achieving your primary goals of success.

The second step in Mind-Set Technologies is known as the Mind-Set Adjustment (MSA), which entails developing constructive habits to replace your destructive ones and establishing more effective thought patterns for a happier, more fulfilling way of living.

According to one dictionary I read years ago, the definition of *technology* is *the study, development, and application of devices, machines, and techniques for manufacturing and productive processes* or *a method or methodology that applies technical knowledge or tools.*

From this definition of *technology*, some of the key words that you can use to apply these exercises to **Mind-Set Technologies are: *Study*, *Develop*, and *Apply*.** Study, develop, and apply methods and techniques to accomplish something of magnificent worth. Let's take a closer look at each of these three key words with respect to **Mind-Set Technologies:**

Study. There is a great need to scrutinize and evaluate your current mind-sets and compare them to your primary goals. Conduct an MSE of where you are on the spectrum of success. Are these mind-sets congruent with achieving good results to lasting joy and happiness? Focus on the mind- sets that are in harmony with your primary goals so you can move forward toward success.

Develop. Exercise and train your mind to adjust to more positive things and ideals and discard the negative. Practice and develop good MSE and MSA skills to get yourself on the road to true success.

Apply. Apply the tools to develop a positive mental attitude and adjust your mind-sets with respect to sustainable joy and happiness to help you stay on the path that leads to true success.

The MSE process needs to be an honest and deliberate way to evaluate your current habits and mind-sets. It is a process to verify whether or not your current habits and mind-sets are aligned with where you want to end up in life. Many times your habits and mind-sets are not aligned with your primary goals. Therefore, you need to make important critical MSAs to get yourself on the right pathway.

What Is a Mind-Set?

So, what is a *mind-set* and what does it have to do with success? According to another dictionary, a *mind-set* is the following:

> A set of assumptions, methods or notations held by one or more people or groups of people, which is so established that it creates a powerful incentive within these people or groups to continue to adopt or accept prior behaviors, choices or tools. This phenomenon of **cognitive bias** is also sometimes described as **mental inertia**, group think, or a paradigm, and it is often **difficult to counteract** its effects upon analysis and decision making process.

According to this definition, in general terms, a mind-set is more than just a train of thought. Rather, it is an effective sustained manner of thinking, acting, and living that will likely lead to results, either positive or negative. MSAs give you an additional mental thrust that is difficult to thwart or turn back as decisions are made, habits are formed, and life courses are set. MSAs are course-setting adjustments that not only get you on the right path but also keep you there. Consider the phases above in the definition that have been bolded: **Cognitive bias, mental inertia, and difficult to counteract and then think of the potential power of transcending and magnificent mind-sets in your life.**

To change from ineffective or destructive mind-sets to transcending mind-sets, you will need to consider, embrace, and bond.

- Consider the concept of the mind-set.

- Embrace the mind-set.
- Bond with the mind-set.

Embracing and bonding with powerful, transcending, and magnificent mind-sets enables you to claim and adopt the mind-set. Then you can use it along your pathway to sustainable success leading to joy and happiness.

Mind-Set Technologies and the Power of PMA

Roger, your MSAs also need to be the kind that will breathe more optimism into your life. Optimism gives you the power of a Positive Mental Attitude (PMA). PMA is the substance, the *power pavement*, that builds an enduring highway to success. PMA-oriented MSAs give you the edge over the common and ordinary ways of thinking that lead to mediocrity. PMA is the missing link to most people's plans for success.

In life's battles, PMA can be thought of as that extra arrow in your quiver that will help you conquer your formidable enemies. The PMA arrow is symbolically constructed with a pure silver shaft for strength and durability; a razor-sharp, diamond-hard arrowhead for ultimate piercing capabilities; and feathers made from angels' wings for guidance and accuracy in delivering your arrow to its desired target—a perfect bull's-eye! PMA delivers the thrust, impact, and accuracy needed to give you the edge over the entropies of this world and win over them. And just like Legolas in the Epic Trilogy, *Lord of the Rings*, who never seemed to run out of arrows in his battles in life, your PMA arrows will never run out as long as you keep andexerciseyour optimistic PMA power.

Upon finishing reading the second section of Billy's writings, Roger was again enlightened and filled with knowledge. He felt a renewed determination to learn how he could adjust his mind-sets to a more positive framework. He had essentially stared death in the face twice that day and was overwhelmed by the fortuitous timing and manner in which the mysterious visitor, whom he now knew was Billy Haynes, had helped him survive.

Following dinner, cleanup, and managing his notes and his field samples, Roger sat down in a comfortable green wooden Adirondack chair on the hardwood deck outside of the Haynes cabin. As darkness fully engulfed the south end of Prince of Wales Island, he gazed in wonder at the white band of the Milky Way and the billions of stars that were visible in a moonless sky. He spotted the North Star and then recognized all the familiar constellations: the Big Dipper, the Little Dipper, Orion, Scorpius, Taurus, Cassiopeia, and several others.

Being the spiritually-minded person that he was, Roger began pondering the mysteries of the universe and God's role as the master planner and creator of it all. Also, as a geologist, he understood something of earth's dynamic systems and knew in his heart that there had to be a divine design and creation to the beauty and complexity of the earth and the cosmos.

Thinking about these wonders of this world land the universe gave Roger the ability to know absolutely that they couldn't have simply flared into existence by simple chance or a series of coincidental accidents. That night, with all that he had experienced earlier that day, and with all that he had read by courtesy of a strange visitor, Roger knew in his heart that he was being watched over and taught by divine intervention. He also knew that this mysterious visitor had some mysterious but real connection with the heavens to provide such miraculous gifts of protection and enlightenment.

Roger also started recalling the lively conversations that he'd had just days ago with the young and prideful Dr. Brundy and truly felt sorry for him going through his sudden illness and surgery earlier that week. But he was even more sorrowful for the contempt Brundy had for those who believed in and loved God.

Feeling humility and gratitude for the joy that he felt when he contemplated the divine creations of the universe and the love of God for all humankind, Roger retired for the night in comfort and with a glad heart.

During the night, Roger had a vivid and enlightening dream involving the Magnificent MindSet Man as a three-dimensional figurine that brightly illuminated and floated in the dark of night. In the dream, Roger was standing on the porch of the Haynes cabin as the Magnificent Mind-Set Man slowly moved closer and closer to him, staring at him face-to-face and eye-to-eye. Then the bright figurine stopped within ten feet of Roger and turned slightly to the right. The BTW piece was illuminated with a violet glow and began flashing like a neon light. Then a beam of pure white light emanated from the Magnificent Mind-Set Man's right eye socket. The beam pointed in the direction of one of the dilapidated mine vehicles, located a few hundred feet up the trail from the Haynes cabin. The vehicle was an old, rusted yellow jeep. As if hypnotized, Roger followed the beam to the jeep. As he approached the vehicle and opened the passenger door, the glove compartment fell open, exposing one of the key cards Roger had found in the chest in the underground mine. It was the violet card. As Roger reached for it, he suddenly awoke from his dream in the Haynes cabin.

Roger remembered the dream in all its details. Looking over to his left side of the night stand, he peered at the bright red numbers illuminated on the clock; the time read: 0445. Immediately, he got out of bed, turned on the light, and found his backup flashlight, which was working perfectly. He put on his field boots and his coat. Once he walked out of the cabin, his breath, which met the night's cold air, produced a stream of vapor, indicating that the nighttime temperatures were starting to dip down into the low to mid-40s Fahrenheit. As Roger pointed his light up the mining road a few feet, he spotted the yellow jeep and immediately approached the car. He opened the passenger's-side door and the glove box, and to his excitement found the violet key card, which he immediately took with him back to the cabin.

Roger was too tired to open the safe and read anything new that early in the morning. Instead, he left the violet key card on the dining room table and climbed back into bed and got another two hours of restful sleep.

CHAPTER 6

MIND-SET 1: YOU WERE BORN TO WIN

Wednesday, September 27 (Expedition - Day 3):
The Violet Key Card

When the 0700 alarm woke Roger, he felt refreshed and invigorated from the good night's rest, despite the dream that had awakened him and the trip out to the jeep just about two hours earlier.

Roger used the violet key card to open the safe as he had with the two other cards. As expected, he found several additional pages to study. But instead of the Magnificent Mind-Set Man figurine, there was something new.

The new figurine, made of pure white porcelain, was in the shape of two caring hands gently holding an infant child, as if they were the hands of God offering a new and precious gift to the world and to the infant's mother, just like the image he had seen the day before in the cave.

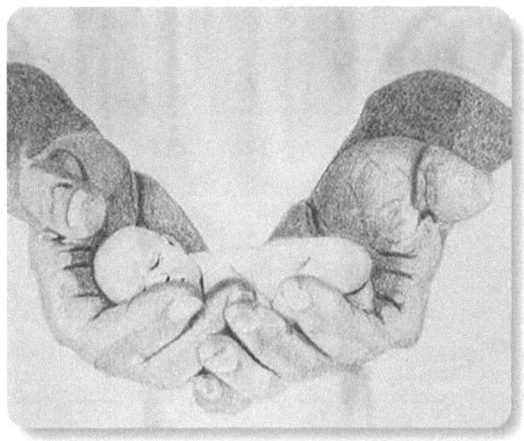

Roger prepared breakfast. As began eating, he started reading the additional BHIII memoirs that were also in the safe that morning.

MSA 1: You Were Born to Win because You Are a God-Child

Roger, evaluate how you currently feel about God and your relationship to him. Conduct an MSE on how you perceive your relationship with the Divinity. If for some reason you do not believe there is a God or that you are somehow related to a God or Supreme Being who loves you and is actively involved in your life, you may have a more difficult time achieving enduring success. An MSA may be in order to give you more strength by drawing upon the powers of the Divine.

Roger, here is your first and most important MSA: realizing that you are a God-child! In the grand scheme of the universe, you are a spiritual being created in the image of God, who is a perfect and omnipotent being. Therefore, you are invested with divine potential. Know that with God, all things are possible. Possessing the knowledge that you are a God-child, should give you a powerful PMA-based mind-set. Since you are his child, you are blessed by birthright with certain key endowments and talents to help you succeed in life.

One of the more important gifts he has given you is the gift of agency. Therefore, you have the ability to choose your path to success. No person or influence can take this gift of agency away from you. It is only through your own choices to follow destructive influences that you can lose the ability to choose.

This You Were Born to Win MSA will breathe a greater degree of confidence into your spiritual and emotional lungs. It will help you to focus on what you need to do to live a happier life and prepare yourself to return to live with an eternal Father in heaven. And the best part about this MSA is that you can be certain that all of this is true: he wants to grant you this kind of successful life. Be confident that he is interested and invested in you, and that he will do his part to help you succeed as long as you choose to take the right steps and follow his plan for your happiness and success.

Paul the apostle taught the ancient Greeks on Mars Hill about the fact that we are the offspring of God (Acts 17:29). As also taught in the book of Hebrews (12:9), we should give even more reverence to the Father of our spirits (who is our Heavenly Father) than we give to the fathers of our flesh. Despite your challenges in this life, you are his child; therefore, you were born to win and succeed. Think of it in the following way, Roger:

We Are the Children of God

> Yes, we are the children of God,
> And he knew us all before.
> But that's not all; there's more.
> We are his spirit-children.
> Since we were truly created
> In his image, you might say
> We are indeed related.
> His grace, his mercy, and love,
> And all good things from above
> Will all be revealed
> When all that he has promised
> Shall at length be fulfilled.

Since you are a God-child, you should now begin to believe that you were indeed born to succeed in this life by winning the great battles you experience on a day-to-day basis. Strive to use this knowledge as a tool. Create and embrace a MSA that will empower you by knowing that ***you were born to win*** and experience a new way of thinking and walking on the pathway to success.

Roger, written below are a few verses to help you bring this MSA into greater focus:

You Were Born to Win

> Life is a battle, but you were born to win.
> Believe it! Say it! And repeat it again!
> This world is a challenge—it does seem rough—
> But now is the time to choose to be tough.
> With all of the strife and struggles and crime,
> You are the one who can awake the divine.
> The divine is within you; the power is strong,
> The ability to conquer the bad and the wrong.
> The struggles are out there; some are within.
> Face them! Beat them, and learn how to win!
> This world is indifferent. Although it may seem
> People are cruel, don't let 'em destroy your dream.
> But you have the power to act and be bold,
> To overcome great trials, no matter how old.
> Give up addictions; they aren't so nice.
> Never be a slave to a substance or vice.
> You are the master, the commander of life.
> You are the one who can temper the strife,
> The strife that is out there and the strife within,
> The strife that we battle. Learn to laugh and grin.
> Overcome the negative with a positive mind.
> Turn con into pro; turn all madness to kind.
> When you get down and are in the blues,
> Rise up and be counted and get enthused.
> You have the smarts and you have the will.
> Use your talents to counter the deal.

Upon reading and contemplating the First Transcending Mind of Success, You Were Born to Win, Roger appreciated the simplicity and reality of the idea that humankind is essentially the spiritual offspring of a Divine and Supreme Being. As simple as this concept was to him, he thought it was a very bold statement that we are all God-children. It was intuitive to Roger, as a student of the Bible, knowing divine teachings as recorded in the book of Acts and the Epistle to the Hebrews, that this was true: God was the Father of his spirit. However, it was an intriguing and transcending concept that he and all human beings had divine gifts and innate endowments inherited from the heavenly realms above.

Roger further pondered the idea that every human being was the offspring of God and, furthermore, part of a divine family. *Each of us is endowed with divine gifts, and each human is a unique creation of God,* Roger said aloud. *Therefore, each person has different divine gifts and different portions of those gifts to help him or her succeed in life.* With all of these new and exciting thoughts, Roger concluded that he could call these gifts, **innate divine talents.**

In addition, the crowning collective gift could best be understood as the gift of agency, or the ability to choose a path that would allow a person to succeed by choice, or choose not to follow constructive paths and thus, forfeit success by default. Roger was completely intrigued by the boldness of Billy's thesis, that humankind's mission in this life is to succeed and prosper in each of the components that make up the human soul.

Following his reading, Roger suddenly realized it was now about 0800 Wednesday on Bokan Mountain, the day that Tyler and Selos were to fly back the Bokan Marina to pick up the samples he had collected during the first two days of his field investigations. Moments later, the voice of Dr. Keiffer Selos came in loud and clear over the ham radio: *Thunder Chicken to Hunt! Thunder Chicken to Hunt! Do you read me, Hunt?*

Roger approached the radio and replied, *Hunt here.*

The voice on the radio said, *Roger, we are about thirty to thirty-five minutes out. Are you ready for us?*

Yes, I am, Selos. I am here and ready for you.

Roger quickly readied all the samples, the signed chain-of-custody forms, and the laboratory protocol for his two clients to pick up and fly back to Northern Lights Analytical Laboratories in Ketchikan.

In addition to picking up the samples, Tyler and Selos were also planning to discuss the initial findings of Roger's environmental investigations, what initial conclusions Roger might have drawn regarding the locations and the potential magnitude of contamination at the Tyler-Haynes Mine. Roger also needed to be prepared to discuss what environmental liabilities may lie in wait for his client, MMI. The final agenda item was to discuss the scope of Roger's work during the next six days of the expedition.

Promptly at 0835, the *Thunder Chicken* landed and Tyler and Selos quickly unloaded and hiked over to the Haynes cabin. Roger, hearing their approach, landing, and arrival, welcomed his two clients and invited them in.

Upon entering the cabin, Tyler started with his usual sarcasm. *Well, Hunt, it's good to see you alive and well. We are truly impressed that you survived the first part of your field investigation.*

Before getting into the items of business, Roger asked Tyler and Selos how the young Dr. Brundy was recovering. A sober, awkward silence followed while Tyler and Selos looked at each other and exchanged some facial expressions and hand gestures, apparently in an effort to gather their thoughts and determine how to respond to Roger's question.

After a couple of moments of further nonverbal communication involving shoulder shrugging and head tilting, Tyler finally formulated a response. *Well... ah, he's finally out of the woods; he should survive.*

Roger looked perplexed. *What do you mean, should survive? I thought this was a routine procedure. He was recovering and doing well when I left the hospital on Sunday night. What the heck happened after we left?*

Selos quickly chimed in. *Yeah, he had some kind of strange reaction to the anesthetics several minutes into his recovery and flat-lined. Brundy was clinically dead for over thirty minutes before he revived. Then he was in a coma for the next twenty-eight hours! He's improved dramatically since then. His surgeons think it was a miracle that he didn't suffer any brain damage. We didn't even hear about all this until Monday afternoon after we got back from dropping you off here on Bokan.*

Tyler then added some additional and strange details. *He only started talking last night, mumbling something like, Where's Hunt? I need to talk to Hunt! Tell him I saw the light, but I didn't go to it—they sent me back! Those glorious men in white in robes sent me back. They told me to go to Roger Hunt and describe this experience to him. Tell Hunt I want to talk to him when he gets back from Bokan.*

Oh my Lord! Roger shouted.

Yeah, literally! mumbled Selos. And then he added, *You never know! You never know!*

Roger added, *Well, I'm glad he didn't go! He's too young to die. It's good to know that he's going to make it through okay. It sounds like he and I will have some interesting things to talk about when I get back.*

After a few silent moments, Selos, in his quasi-professional way, said, *well, Roger, we trust that you've enjoyed the work so far and that you have been able to document each of the environmental conditions out there and collect all the samples necessary to complete your study.*

Roger quickly returned to business. *Yes. Here are all the samples in these ice chests, both soil and water, and the paperwork is all ready for your receipt, signature, and final submittal to the laboratory.*

Selos then turned to Tyler and winked sarcastically. Turning back to Roger, he said, *Very good, Hunt. Very good, my friend!*

Over the next several minutes, Roger sat with Tyler and Selos at the dining room table and thoroughly reviewed the results of Hunt's findings to make sure that the scope of his work so far was complete according to everyone's satisfaction.

Then the team reviewed the arduous tasks ahead. Those activities would include recording radiological readings with a handheld instrument called a scintillation counter. The scintillation counter, or scintillometer, would be used to measure the qualitative radiological activity of residual mining waste rock in storage and loading areas, the openings of the various underground and open-pit mines, and the various mining roads where the rock was used as a base to reduce road erosion.

As they concluded the meeting and planned for the final pickup on the following Tuesday at the Tyler cabin, a good eight miles away from the Haynes cabin, Tyler suddenly turned back to ask Roger one final question: *Anything else interesting happen here the last couple of days, Hunt?*

Roger thought for a moment and then replied with some sarcasm of his own: *If you're asking whether or not I've had any Billy Haynes sightings, then I must be truthful and say yes. I have indeed both seen and heard from Mr. Haynes himself, at least twice in the last day or two.*

Oh, really? Selos perked up with unbelieving excitement at this revelation. Then he looked back at Tyler with a childish grin on his face as if to beg for some fun and entertaining stories and tales.

So you met Billy, have you? Tyler piped up with a chuckle. *Tell us all about it, Hunt. We're all ears!* Selos started laughing under his breath.

Yeah, well, he, he—uh, he saved my life just yesterday from Chloe, replied Roger.

A moment of silence again prevailed. Tyler's jaw dropped wide open in amazement. He looked at Selos, who lifted his eyebrows high above his glasses. The two geo-businessmen just stared at each other without saying a word.

Roger, unable to take the silence any longer, blurted out, *What? What did I say?*

Tyler started murmuring in the way he usually did when he was trying to find the right words. *Well ... ah, Chloe is what Billy used to call each of the female black bears on the island. He named them after his favorite dog, Chloe, a black Labrador that he trained to perform a variety of fun tricks, including fetching the morning newspaper each day, and that he used to jog with throughout the years. But the question is, Roger, how would you have known that?*

Hey, read the writing on the wall: Billy was here. Roger referred to a knife-carved phrase engraved into one of the logs of the north wall of the Haynes cabin, which read, *Billy to Chloe, my beloved dog, who mothered eight black pups, just like all the great mother bears on this beautiful island.*

Wow, that's corny, what a strange eulogy from a strange man, Roger concluded.

Then, after a second or two, the three of them burst out in a round of laughter and patted each other on their backs like old college fraternity brothers.

Then Tyler and Selos suddenly grabbed the sample chests and all the paperwork and quickly headed straight for the *Thunder Chicken* without another word about Billy Haynes.

As the copter started up and the two men began to slowly ascend, Tyler yelled out to Roger, *See ya Tuesday, Hunt! And stay away from those bears! Roger waved them off as he saw their silent laughter amid the roar and rising of the Thunder Chicken.*

Roger spent the rest of the day taking and recording radiological readings with the scintillometer around the base of the Tyler-Haynes Mine and along the mine road headed toward the underground mine areas. He wanted to stay close to the Haynes cabin in case he encountered Chloe again, but he felt somewhat confident that Billy had taken care of the aggravated mother bear for a while.

When Roger was heading back to the Haynes cabin at the end of the field day, he saw from a hundred yards away that a man was just closing the cabin door and leaving the premises. It looked like Billy Haynes; he was wearing those same old tan pants with his long-sleeve shirt, field boots, and ranger-style hat.

Roger was eager to meet him, but he was also a little reluctant, given that whenever he had either heard Billy's voice or seen him, there was usually something bad associated with his presence.

Nonetheless, Roger called out to the man; *Billy! Billy! Dr. Haynes?*

There was no response back from Billy; he just kept walking briskly in the opposite direction, down the path, and slowly disappearing off to the east end of the mine proper and into the thick forest, too far away for Roger to have any hope of catching up to him.

As Roger got to the cabin, he strongly suspected there would be a new key card to access the safe, a new figurine, and fresh set of pages to study that evening during dinner and relaxation time.

He was right. This time the key was indigo, just like the one he had lost in the underground mine the day before.

CHAPTER 7

MIND-SET 2: UNDERSTAND AND NULLIFY ENTROPY

Wednesday, September 27 (Expedition - Day 3 [contd]): The Indigo Key Card

Later that night, Roger used the indigo key to open the safe. He reached in pulled out a three-inch-in- diameter metallic figurine of a red apple with a bite taken out of each side.

The new set of writings read as follows:

Understand and Nullify the Negative Effects of Entropy

Roger, the second magnificent MSA that will inspire you and encourage you to be more successful is the MSA called *Understand and Nullify the Negative Effects of Entropy*.

The application of this MSA will help keep you off the pathway of frustration and will give you the ability to outsmart and consciously overcome the natural state of the world, which is **entropy,** or the corrupting and decaying tendency of the world in which we all live.

According to the second law of thermodynamics, entropy is the natural process of changing from a higher-ordered state to a lower-ordered state. The higher the degree of entropy you experience, the higher degree of a disordered state you will experience.

In a nonscientific way, I have chosen to use the word *entropy* to illustrate a way of perceiving the natural state and conditions of the world in which we all live.

Entropy is both your enemy and your friend. From a religious standpoint, entropy, I suppose would be the result of the fall of Adam and Eve, our first parents on this earth. It means that anything and everything decays and tends toward disease, death, and corruption.

Entropy, for the purposes of this exercise could also be considered all those nagging things that discourage you on earth. Development and application of this positive and life-transforming MSA is a key and critical process along the pathway to success and happiness. Recognize entropy and combat it; live with it and overcome its negative effects as much as possible with positive actions. This process was designed to test and strengthen you and create opportunities to work to overcome and grow. Consider how important the concept of work is to our health and sanity in this otherwise corrupt world.

Since the fall of Adam, we have been living in an *indifferent mortal world*. The natural state of this earth is disorder. My children were a great example of this concept of disordered state. When they were still alive, all I had to do was walk into their rooms and witness entropy and disorder.

You should know this too, Roger, because you also have kids. When little kids are in the house, your home goes from a high state of order to a low state of order in sixty seconds flat. Out come all the toys, and then all over the floor they go, in a state of chaos and disorder.

Other examples of entropy are the day-to-day challenges you experience in life.

You can do a great job of landscaping your yard, but unless you keep it up by mowing your lawn regularly, watering your lawn and garden, and applying weed-and-feed to your lawn and physically weeding your garden, things will get out of control really fast and weeds and other overgrowth will take over.

If you neglect to provide for the appropriate maintenance to your home, your car, and other important things, nature will take control and things will break down and waste away.

If you don't watch what you eat, you will gain weight, get really fat, and develop all kinds of diseases that will lead to a lower quality of life and even cause an early death. You can lose weight and get in tip-top shape, but if you don't keep up with your diet and exercise routine, you will lose your muscle tone, put on more unwelcome weight, and be out of shape in no time at all.

If you are a man and do not shave regularly, you will grow a beard, and if you don't actively trim your beard, it won't take long for it to look pretty raggedy and scruffy.

If you don't learn, you will stay ignorant and fail to progress intellectually.

If you don't keep learning, your mind will waste away faster than you think.

If you don't stay current with technology, you will get left behind in a world that is changing at an ever-increasing rate.

How Do We Combat the Negative Effects of Entropy?

Basically, there are three kinds of people in the world:

1. Those who make things happen
2. Those who watch things happen
3. Those who wonder, *what happened?*

Which kind are you, Roger? Which do you want to be?

You have learned the importance of setting primary goals so as to know what you are shooting for to achieve sustainable success. Likewise, setting supporting goals to achieve a primary goal is important to make you more effective, if you set these goals in relation to the *whole soul of humankind*, which consists of the following components:

- the heart – the spiritual side of a man or woman
- might – the emotional side of a man or woman
- the mind – the mental side of a man or woman
- strength – the physical side of a man or woman
- the social side of a man or woman

Goals need to be set if you are to improve yourself in each of these main areas and provide the appropriate balance in life.

One way to think of this *whole-soul-of-man* concept in terms of setting goals is to segregate each of the five components into five different buckets, as follows:

- the spiritual bucket
- the emotional bucket
- the mental bucket
- the physical bucket
- the social bucket

If you are lacking progress in any of these five whole-soul buckets, or if any of your buckets are empty or nearly empty, you may be shorting yourself on some of the effective tools at your disposal to conquer your most formidable enemies. Roger, please remember that each of us is responsible for either filling or emptying any or all of these whole-soul buckets.

Another important note is that each of us may be born with greater or lesser capacities in our whole-soul buckets. Because of deficiencies in genetics and a world dominated by entropy, some people may be born with certain physical, mental, or emotional limitations that may result in handicaps and impairments. Most of us will have life challenges, either great or small, because of lowervolume whole-soul buckets that arise as the result of inheritance, illnesses, accidents, or choice.

Also, some people are born with large volumes for their physical, mental, and emotional buckets and are thus blessed with different gifts or talents. As we grow and age, each of us is responsible for evaluating and doing the best we can to balance our whole-soul buckets.

By your neglect, ignorance, or negative actions, you can drain any one of these buckets. Or, by positive actions and perseverance in setting and achieving goals in each of these areas, you can fill these buckets to create a more healthy, happy, and successful life.

A car can only run well with all four tires fully inflated, in good shape, and with plenty of tread to grip the road, especially in rain, snow, or ice. It only takes one tire having a flat to knock the car off the path, and a blowout could put you in peril.

A spare tire in your trunk can be thought of as a fifth element to the whole soul of a man or woman: the social component.

I believe that in life, nothing good happens by itself; therefore, if you do nothing, nothing good will happen.

The world is waiting for something good to happen and for someone like you, Roger, who is willing to be bold, take a chance, and make something good happen! The world is counting on you, Roger, to be proactive and take control of life's situations.

You can make good things happen!

You can make a difference in this world!

Think of yourself as being a good thing in this world that is otherwise dominated by entropy, decay, and disorder. Be enthusiastic about the millions of opportunities that are out there for you to seize upon. It is up to you to embrace this mind-set so that you can go out and make a real difference in the world!

The challenges, struggles, temptations, and setbacks that you face in life, as strange as it may sound, are a gift and a blessing to you. The very process of struggling and overcoming your challenges, no matter how difficult, helps build faith, character, and self-esteem, and gives you the willpower to carry on along your pathway to success. A key element to your quest for success in life is the ability to make the MSAs that you need to make in order to overcome and battle your way through your challenges, struggles, and adversities and thereby conquer, learn, and win.

If you do not think you have challenges in life, then maybe your lack of challenges is your biggest challenge.

Think of your challenges as gifts and blessings to help you grow, not as burdens and stumbling blocks that get in the way of your success. **The person who is never challenged or has never failed is the same person who has never been given the opportunity to truly grow and progress toward success.**

The rule here is that you cannot change the mind-sets of others and others cannot effectively or permanently change your mind-sets. If you want to change or adjust your mind-sets, you have to learn to do it yourself. If you want a new mind-set, you need to find it and develop it. You might be greatly influenced or motivated by others, and rightly so, but when it comes right down to it, it is really you that can change your mind-sets.

The point here is, stop loitering about and get on the ball. Be anxiously engaged in doing good things for your family, others, and yourself. Think on the moral of the tale *The Golfer and the Ants*.

The Golfer and the Ants

Once there was a golfer who could not see
Quite as well as you or as well as me.
With his bad vision, he took a failed swing.
He missed the ball badly. It was no big thing.
He swung once, and then he swung twice.
He missed it again; he was as cold as ice.
He could not see the ball; he did not make the hit.
Instead he cut a hole that golfers call a divot.
He did not notice that in the big crater he'd made
'Twas a colony of ants, and in there they stayed.
With his third swing, the ants only numbered a few.

> Then on the fourth swing, all that were left were two,
> Two little ants, each like a brother.
> *I know what!* said one to the other.
> *If we are to be saved, we should not stand here at all.*
> *The one thing that will save us is this: let's get on the ball!*

After Roger had finished reading the concepts presented in MSA 2, he began to evaluate how he could relate to these new ideas. Dozens of examples of how entropy had negatively affected him throughout the years started coming to mind. However, examples of the very conditions around him at the Tyler-Haynes Mine began to dominate his thinking.

It was interesting and obvious to Roger how, after the disappearance of Billy Haynes around the end of the Cold War in the late 1980s, the TylerHaynes Mine was suddenly abandoned and all the structures, equipment, and supplies were just left to slowly canker and become a disorganized eyesore. Thereafter, nature proceeded to swallow up everything man-made. Everything was left on its own to be acted upon by the law of entropy—to decay and rot in its place. *These are classic examples of entropy,* Roger thought to himself.

Roger also started thinking of the different physical and environmental hazards at the various mining and support areas around Bokan Mountain. Neglect and humankind's disturbance of these areas had caused these hazards. Everyday hazards were out there in the real world, either the result of nature or the result of the neglect and carelessness of human beings.

If people were careless and allowed themselves to embrace things like drugs, tobacco, alcohol, gambling, sex addictions including pornography, and other substances and vices, then these negative things could accelerate entropy in their lives and become the dominant part of their thoughts, actions, and character, eventually destroying them. First people experimented with these vices, then they enjoyed them, then they embraced them, and then they bonded with them, which was essentially addiction and the process of enslaving themselves to the substance or vice. Thereafter, their ability to exercise their agency was damaged, compromised, or diminished.

Roger also began to draw analogies of these mining hazards to real-life tragedies. Exposure to poisonous radon gas, falls, and cave-ins were analogous to falling into dangerous traps related to bad habits and addictions. Other hazards, such as being overexposed to radioactive waste rock and other materials in the old ore storage and loading areas, were also analogous to the addictions people oftentimes had fallen into and could not easily escape.

The entropies that affect everyone were there as part of the real world. You can accelerate the negative aspects of entropy by falling into bad habits and eventual addictions. However, the negative aspects of entropy can be overcome with positive action; in other words, work, and the formation of good habits (thus replacing the bad habits). These include such efforts as physical and creative activities and service to others—*essentially staying sober by rendering habits and addictions irrelevant and eventually getting rid of the bad habits and addictions altogether. Making the bad habits and addictions irrelevant is the key to overcoming these negative influences,* Roger concluded.

The ability to overcome the negative effects of entropy depended on personal commitment to setting and achieving personal goals to improve in each of the five whole-soul components of humankind: physical, spiritual, emotional, mental, and social.

Roger reflected upon these thoughts in a personal way and became convinced that his life up to this point would have been much better if he had been more proactive and diligent in setting and achieving goals. He reflected on how he'd neglected opportunities to set goals in each of the whole-soul areas and how he could have made improvements that would have inured him against falling into many bad habits with their subsequent negative effects.

He started laying out a plan to set goals and improve in these areas, but soon he grew tired from all of the day's activities. He decided to get some sleep for the night and get a fresh start in the morning, refocusing on his goal-setting quest during breakfast for a few quality minutes before returning to the field.

During the night, Roger began dreaming again. The Mind-Set Man stared at him and spoke telepathically: *Be F.A.I.R. to yourself, Roger! Learn the F.A.I.R. principles of goal setting, and win!*

This message was repeated three times. Simultaneously, the F.A.I.R. puzzle piece was illuminated on both sides of the head of the Mind-Set Man as the image pivoted from side to side. The illumination immediately turned indigo. Then suddenly, the Mind-Set Man turned to the left, and as before, a beam of pure white light shone from its left eye and rested upon the waters of the marina just beyond the heliport platform. As Roger started following this light to the point where it entered the water, he noticed that the beam focused on a familiar object: the box that he had found in the underground mine two days before that carried the key cards. Just when he was about to enter the water to retrieve the box, his 0700 alarm went off, waking him from his slumber at the crack of dawn.

CHAPTER 8

MIND-SET 3: BE F.A.I.R. TO YOURSELF

Thursday, September 28 (Expedition - Day 4):
The Blue Key Card

Roger awoke with this most recent dream firmly fixed in his mind. He immediately got dressed and went straight out to the marina heliport. He saw a shiny colored object sparkling in the morning sunlight. Finding a shovel nearby, he used it to retrieve the object from the crystal clear water. He found a hand towel from the Haynes cabin and used it to dry off the metallic object. It was a one of the lost key cards: the blue one that he had seen and held in his hands two days before.

Roger immediately took the blue key card back into the cabin and used it to open the safe, in which he found a new metallic figurine consisting of a round magnifying glass, the acronym *F.A.I.R.* engraved in the center. As before, new pages had been added to the folder.

Roger prepared breakfast. As he ate, he read on:

Be F.A.I.R. to Yourself

With respect to setting and establishing your primary or supporting goals, learn the F.A.I.R. principles:

    F: Focus
    A: Attitude
    I: Investment
    R: Relevance

Focus

Proper focus will help you achieve your goals. Focus on your strengths, your talents, and your divine gifts. Focus on the goodness of your goals, and note how by achieving those goals you can succeed at the important things of life.

Focus on your goals with particular interest on your strengths. Strive to focus on the importance and essence of why you have set any primary or supporting goal and the likelihood of obtaining success through accomplishment of your goals. Filter out unwanted influences, and hone in on those that are in harmony with your goals.

Attitude

An optimistic attitude gives you the power of a Positive Mental Attitude (PMA). PMA is the substance, the *power pavement*, that builds an enduring highway to success. PMA-oriented MSAs give you the edge over the common and ordinary ways of thinking that lead to mediocrity. As I said before, PMA is the missing link to most people's plan for success and its execution.

As presented earlier in my second memoir (see chapter 5), PMA can and should play an important and powerful role in your life. Roger, if only you would capture the mental image of pulling that proverbial PMA arrow out of the quiver of your mind and letting it fly with confidence to slay each of your bad habits, doubts, fears one at a time. You need to be patient with yourself and take it one step at a time, but make steady progress each new day of your life. Take on the smaller and easier-to-overcome bad habits, replacing them with easy good habits (such as making your bed as soon as you get up). Then incrementally graduate to your more formidable challenges and strive to replace those bad habits with more difficult good habits and positive traits (such as learning to manage stress or having highly effective time-management skills).

The key is to stay enthusiastic and positive as you make progress with something each day. And reward yourself with an emotional and mental motion picture of all the onlookers and fans cheering you on and applauding your victories. Can you picture that in your mind, Roger? How does that make you feel to hear the crowd roaring and cheering you on as you succeed? Doesn't that feel great?

Investment

Invest time, talents, divine gifts, resources, and finances in your primary and supporting goals so that your proverbial bank account to finance your success is fully funded. How much time and effort do you take to assess, study, and determine the most important primary or ultimate goals and supporting goals? Once you focus in on and set worthwhile goals, how much time do you spend on writing them down in a journal or recording them in some other formal way? Do you share your goals with your family, friends, and work associates? Do you invest time and resources in planning out activities, events, and schedules that are focused around your goals? For goals to be realized, you will have to make them the center of the things that you should be doing on a day-to-day basis.

For a person to make her bank account and retirement portfolios grow, she must financially invest in those funds. For a professional investor to succeed in the markets, she needs to not only invest money but also take time to study the markets and know her clients' needs. She needs to study growth patterns of the strategic markets and know which markets are the ones that are heading in the directions that are consistent with her business plan. She needs to quickly know when to get in and when to get out, when to alert her clients to do the same, when to keep things diversified, and when to narrow in on fewer key markets.

For your goals portfolio, do you regulate how much time and effort you need to spend on improving your whole soul in physical, mental, emotional, spiritual, and social terms? Maybe the need to focus more time and effort on one of these areas becomes acute. For instance, maybe you learn from a medical exam that because you are overweight, maintain a poor diet, and take very little or no time to exercise, you are on the brink of developing diabetes, and if you do not take some corrective action to change your habits and focus, your health will soon take a turn in a direction you have always feared but now know is possible. Given these circumstances, you need to take the time to study the literature your physician gives you and decide to make some course-changing habits. Essentially, you are in need of some MSEs and MSAs to effectively get yourself on the right track physically.

Because of this imbalance in your life, it behooves you to invest your time and financial resources into saving your body from irrevocable damage. You plan out and invest in a better diet and take the time to get more exercise to help eliminate or alleviate the negative effects of poor health.

So you may say, *But I don't have any physical problems in my life*. If that is the case, then maybe your goal is to keep forming good habits or to make the preventative changes now to avoid future poor health. It was the ever wise Benjamin Franklin who once said that *an ounce of prevention is worth a pound of cure*. How true that statement is, especially more than two hundred years later, and how important it is for you to make investments in good health—your physical, spiritual, mental, emotional, and social health.

Relevance

Keep the focus on your goals by sticking with what is relevant. Apply the relevance filter: systematically filter everything else out of your life (visable and audible stimuli) that would be a distraction to your goals and keep you off the path to success. Let the more relevant things become louder and more prominent in your life, thus playing more of a positive role in your life and leading to the achievement of your goals. As you filter out the irrelevant and distracting things, they become less prominent, fade into the background, and dwindle away from your focus, and thus they are less of a problem. Think about having your own volume control over the influences of your life. Think of having the ability to turn up the relevance dial for the things that you want to listen to and to turn the dial down for the less relevant things in order to make the negative influences fade away and effectively disappear from your senses.

After finishing breakfast and his morning readings, Roger carefully prepared his field pack for the day with lunch, a field notebook, site maps, the .44 Magnum (in case he met up with Chloe again—or any of the other five hundred black bears on the island), a first aid kit, his scintillometer, and other ancillary supplies. As prepared as he could be, Roger left the cabin for the day to resume his radiological assessment of mine waste-rock deposits.

Today his plan was to assess the areas adjacent to the open-pit mining operations, approximately two miles up from the fork in the road that separated the underground mines, an area downhill to the left from the open-pit mines and then uphill to the right. After two hours of strenuous hiking uphill, climbing nearly twelve hundred vertical feet, Roger reached a broad plateau south of the final, steep ascent to the peak of Bokan Mountain.

This area, noted on the map as *Billy's Vista*, was the point where the main mining road suddenly ended and several minor mining roads and trails began, tying together the three principal open-pit mines, one to the west, another to the south, and a third to the east—the Abraham, Isaac, and Jacob open-pit mines, respectively. Each of these three mines was five hundred to six hundred feet long and forty to fifty feet wide. Each had a long and sinuous shape, vertical-cliff sides, and depths ranging from twenty to thirty-five feet.

One other small path continued on to the north, toward the BHIII Vein exploration areas, where many of the unmined rare earth metal deposits were reportedly located.

Being the beautiful, crisp, clear day that it was, with temperatures in the upper fifties and lower sixties, the view from Billy's Vista was spectacular, to say the least. To the south, approximately 1,250 feet below, were the sloping lands painted with dark green trees and lush vegetation. Down there the forested southernmost tip of the island met up against the deep blue Pacific Ocean, and there were several smaller island fragments as far as the eye could see. To the east was a similar view, only enhanced with the shallow marina near the base camp. To the west, the Pacific Ocean was an endless water world of wonder fading away into the horizon. In that direction, it seemed like Roger could see forever.

Roger's favorite view, however, was the 3,996-foot rise to the north as the steep forested slopes leaned toward the bald rocky peak of Bokan Mountain, rising ever so prominently. Each of these views was unique, awe-inspiring, and unforgettable to Roger.

To Roger's surprise, he again heard the startling distant call of the wild from the bald eagle, which rekindled the quiet emotional stir and the subsequent calming effect within his soul that he'd experienced before. This call again initiated Roger's remembrance of all the experiences and learnings from the past few days while on Bokan Mountain.

After a few moments of savoring this repeated experience, Roger resumed his field duties and began reading and recording radiological levels along the mining road toward the open-pit mine areas. While working, he was still able to consider in depth his need to set goals in each of the five whole-soul areas using the applications laid out in the F.A.I.R. principles.

The idea of focusing on the kinds of goals that would greatly enhance his life seemed very practical and appealing to Roger. But he knew that he needed to define and lay out a plan for what goals he was going to focus on and discern how that focus would help him achieve his goals. He created a four-part plan, as follows:

Focus

> *No. 1*
>
> I will write my goals down in a journal, on a chart, or on something I can see, on something in my face, so I can be reminded and have to chance to review, record, and remind myself often, even on a daily basis. These goals should emphasize forming good habits in each of the five whole-soul categories.
>
> *No. 2*
>
> I will make these goals quantifiable or measurable. In other words, I won't just write down, *I'm going to exercise three times a week,* in the physical category. Instead, I will write down something like, *I am going to swim, ride a bike, or run a certain distance three days this week and then increase that distance or duration by a certain amount each week. Then I will do such-and-such repetitions of*

calisthenics (specific types) and/or lifting of weights, push-ups, sit-ups, etc.

Similarly, in the intellectual development area; *I will write down the books I want to read, subjects I want to improve in, or languages that I might want to start learning, and so on. I will focus on the time frame to complete the reading or the study,* asking myself, *How many days of reading or studying do I need to do to complete these tasks?* Of course I will also ask, *Why do I want to read and study these materials, and how can they be expected to enhance my intellectual and mental capacities?*

No. 3

I will share these goals with my spouse, trusted friends, and coworkers so that I will be held accountable. One person might agree to be my designated coach or cheerleader to help me evaluate where I used to be and where I am going with respect to these goals. I might also want to agree to help others and be a coach to someone else who is committed to setting goals.

No. 4

I will evaluate and adjust as I proceed in setting and working on my goals. I will try to determine if progress in each of these areas is worth the effort. I will make sure that these goals are obtainable but also make sure that I am stretching to obtain the goals without making and setting goals that are too high or unrealistic, avoiding early discouragement and an early exit from these goals.

Roger promised himself that he would start simply and watch his progress and associated growth. He would develop a system in which he would reward himself when he had achieved measurable progress or reached certain milestones related to his goals. He could reward himself with something that would help him appreciate the feeling of accomplishment and validation. Recognizing and appreciating selfaccomplishments was a process of **self-reinforcement** that would enhance and enrich his life.

Once Roger got to a point where he began to recognize the good things that were overtaking many of the negative things within him, the world around him would give him a stronger purpose. This process would progressively make Roger stronger and would be a mechanism of self-empowerment that would strengthen him to overcome the entropies of the world.

The F.A.I.R. principles were deeply embedded in Roger's thoughts the rest of the day during his field labors; his preoccupation helped make the day go by quicker than usual. Instead of being a distraction for him during the day's field activities, his ponderings of these truths seemed to give him a greater capacity to work safely, effectively, and efficiently. His mind and soul were enlightened, and he was able to complete his assessments at the Abraham Mine in the morning, have an early lunch, and finish the Isaac and Jacob Mines by 1600.

The way back to the cabin was all downhill. Before long, Roger was in a wood chair at the table, completing his field notes and summary of the radiological conditions at each mine. He continued for the next half hour in his preparations for the next day and then had a simple butfilling dinner.

After dinner, Roger relaxed on the deck in his favorite Adirondack chair. The night air was starting to get colder each day, dipping down into the mid-forties, so Roger wrapped himself in a warm quilted Los Angeles Dodgers blanket that Billy had left in the cabin. That was another thing that Roger liked about Billy Haynes; Roger was a Dodgers.

As Roger kept warm and comfortable outside the Haynes cabin, he continued thinking about and reviewing the kinds of goals he should start working on once he returned to Salt Lake City in the coming week. He vowed to make his quiet Sunday afternoons his time each week to set goals, evaluate the progress he'd made on his goals, and consider new goals or adjustments to previous ones.

He also considered personal applications of the other three F.A.I.R. principles, as follows:

Attitude

Roger knew that keeping a positive mental attitude (PMA) would help him stay confident, motivated, and enthusiastic about his goals.

Investment

Roger considered how he should apportion and schedule the time each Sunday afternoon so that he could invest that time in planning and carrying out his goals, as well as evaluating his finances and his emotions.

Relevance

Roger knew he should keep his focus; he should turn the proverbial volume down for things that were irrelevant to his goals or distracted him from his goals and turn up the volume for things that were relevant and key to achieving goals.

These were the things Roger began to consider, ponder, and apply to his life on that Thursday night in the Haynes cabin on Bokan Mountain. As the night wore on, he began to feel the weight of the day and of all his field activities. He finally fell into a deep sleep in the Adirondack deck chair.

As he slept, Roger again dreamed of being guided by the Magnificent Mind-Set Man, this time through the forest as he followed the figurine uphill toward the open-pit mine area and then back into an area that Roger did not recognize. After what seemed like hours of wading through the trees, the Magnificent Mind-Set Man finally came to rest in a previously unexplored area to the south side of Bokan. As Roger approached the motionless image, he became aware of an opening to an unmapped underground mine covered by dense vegetation, trees, and thick brush. The Magnificent Mind-Set Man suddenly entered the mine. Roger followed without hesitation and without fear, fully trusting his wise and loyal guide.

With its glowing countenance, the Magnificent Mind-Set Man guided Roger for several hundred feet into the mountain and finally came to rest, illuminating the back of the mine. At this point, Roger spotted a familiar object resting upon a large flat rock. He immediately recognized the object as being the same Egyptian alabaster chest that he had found and handled in the first underground mine just a couple of days before. The Magnificent Mind-Set Man's glow provided sufficient light to help Roger open the chest and view its contents, which consisted of the four remaining colored key cards, which he had seen before: the green, the yellow, the orange, and the red. As Roger held the chest snug against his body with his left arm, he grabbed the four cards with his right hand and firmly grasped them, determined not to lose them again. As he did so, he was startled to notice that the figurine was quickly moving toward the front of the mine and exiting the cave. Immediately, Roger began following the Magnificent Mind-Set Man toward the opening.

Then he heard a familiar, terrifying growl of a bear coming toward him from an unknown direction. Roger instantly froze in his tracks, picturing the horror and pain of the bear's claws and fangs shredding his flesh. This awful realization of extreme danger motivated him to sprint toward the entrance of the mine. In his haste, Roger tripped and fell over a rock in the near darkness. Again he dropped the chest, but he continued to grip the key cards in his right hand. Quickly getting up, he noticed that the chest was once again lost to the darkness of a cave. With urgency, he quickly followed the figurine out of the mine and into the forest.

As the figurine vanished into the night, Roger suddenly awoke from his dream and was relieved, realizing he was safely back at the cabin. He noticed that he was still reclined in the Adirondack chair. To Roger's amazement, he was inexplicably still clutching, with white knuckles, the four remaining key cards in his right hand. He wondered if the dream had been real. *If not, then how did I reclaim the key cards?* he questioned himself in amazement and wonder.

He entered the cabin and noticed that the clock read 0310. Roger tried a few times to open the safe with each of the four remaining key cards, but none of them worked. Still tired from being awakened in the middle of the night, he fell into bed to complete his night's sleep. He awoke with his alarm at precisely 0700, refreshed and ready for the new day.

CHAPTER 9

MIND-SET 4: BE *TURNED-OUT* AND WIN

**Friday, September 29 (Expedition - Day 5):
The Green Key Card**

The new morning was producing gray clouds and a gloomy sunrise. Roger noticed that all four of the remaining key cards were still lying on the kitchen table. He decided to continue to follow the order of the remaining cards based on the colors of the rainbow; therefore, he used the green key card to open the safe that morning. Unlike what had happened the night before, the safe opened, as if to tell Roger that only one correct key card would work one day at a time.

Roger was beginning to notice this pattern from the events of the last several days on Prince of Wales Island. Also, he was aware that each day the card from the previous day would mysteriously disappear, proving to him that someone, probably Billy Haynes or his ghost, was carefully orchestrating this daily parade of show-and-tell to educate and edify Roger for a special purpose.

Roger removed the new figurine and a fresh set of BHIII memoirs and began inspecting the new items. The new figurine was a flat metallic ten-inch disk-like object. Its color resembled that of brushed nickel. The disk had a two-inch-diameter center and sixteen curved arrows engraved on it. Every other arrow pointed inward and outward. Eight emanated from the center to the edge of the object, as if pointing outward into infinity. The other eight arrows pointed inward into the same central core, as if coming to an end at the word **SELF**.

Turned-In vs. *Turned-Out* Principles

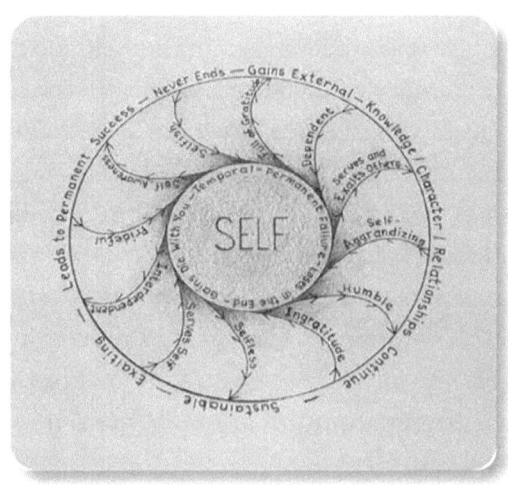

Roger began reading the additional BHIII memoirs.

Be *Turned-Out* and Win

Do something good for others, Roger—every day of your life! This is necessary because nothing good happens on its own.

Roger, learn to be *turned-out* rather than *turned-in*. Lose yourself in being of service of others and gain the best of what this world has to offer. If you will learn the joy of strengthening others, that process will strengthen you. Learn the difference between being *turned-in* and *turned-out*. Conduct an MSE to determine which of the two directions (*turned-out* vs. *turned-in*) dominates your current mind-set.

Are you primarily *turned-in* with respect to your thinking patterns and habits? Or are you *turned-out* ? Do you make yourself the center of attention and the center of your interpersonal relationships? Is everything about you in your conversations with others, or do you reach out in your interactions with others to get to know them and find out about what makes them, them? Do you find out what others need, and do you lend a hand and help when needed?

Being raised a Christian, Roger, you should be well acquainted with the words of Jesus when he taught his disciples that they should lose themselves to the service of others. Matthew 10:39 reads, *He that finds his life shall lose it: and he that loses his life for my sake shall find it.*

Roger, we must trust that this seemingly paradoxical statement is actually true. If you lose your selfish self in the service of others, that very work will bless you and save you. But if you never learn the joy of serving others, or if you feel sorry for yourself and never take time to reach out, then you will remain primarily *turned-in*. If you haven't already, you will someday find that selfishness will lead to bad habits and deleterious character traits, which in turn will lead to self-destruction.

Roger, you must learn to trust the Master's admonition to be *turned-out* more than *turned-in*. The more you serve others, the more you will know that the apparent absurdity of losing yourself to save yourself is truly a reality.

The *Turned-Out* MSA is based on the idea that you have no problems that cannot be solved if you turn outward to help others.

When I am stuck in myself and when my mind is only thinking of myself, my problems, and my own desires, I am *turned-in* on myself. That pattern has an end: the center of my soul. Thus, in that *turned-in* state, any progression of your soul, from either a mortal or an eternal perspective, will also have an end. You will lose friends and family members if you think only of yourself. You will be doomed to live in a lonely and miserable state if you choose to stay *turned-in* toward yourself.

However, if you can find a way out of the *turned-in* state, maybe you can turn things around in your life. The goodness that you naturally have within your heart (because you have somehow been reminded that you are a spirit-child of a divine and perfect Supreme Being) can flow out from you toward others in a never-ending direction: outward and into eternity. By serving and caring for the needy, the widowed, the suffering, and the sad among us, you will naturally and spiritually come to realize that you truly love those whom you serve. You will form eternal bonds in these relationships and receive never-ending blessings that will help define the new you, the *turned-out* you, the *eternity-focused* you.

By reaching out and serving others as Christ served, your problems will be minimized and your character will be strengthened in the very process. The more you serve and learn to love others, the more you will realize that you have no problems that cannot be solved, no challenges that cannot be conquered, and no weakness that cannot be overcome.

Roger, you know people who, despite serious travesties in their lives, have overcome sadness and tragedies and are largely *turned-out*. Please write about each of these people here in the blank pages that follow.

Turned-Out People

Roger, knowing immediately who these people were that Billy was inquiring about, began writing about each his experiences with them, adding examples of their choosing to be *turned-out*.

> *John Flagstaff*
> About five years ago, a friend and former coworker of mine, John Flagstaff, was in a very serious and fiery car accident. His sports car collided with a semi-truck at a very high speed and caught fire with him trapped inside. John was successfully rescued by first responders, but as a result of the accident, he was in a coma for several days.
>
> When I learned of his tragic accident from another coworker a week or two later, I was told that he was recovering well but was burned badly from head to toe. About three weeks after his accident, I decided to pay John a visit in a Denver-area hospital. I reached his floor. While I was looking for his room, I passed several hallways, rooms, and nurses' stations. Then I noticed out of the corner of my eye that a man I did not

recognize was being slowly guided by a nurse on a walk around the main hallway of the floor. At the same time, I found myself essentially lost in my quest to find John's room, so I asked a nurse at the closest nurses' station where I might find John Flagstaff's room.

Room 209, around the corner, she called out. *Tell me your name and I'll ring his room to make sure he is able to see you.*

Roger Hunt, I said.

At that moment, I heard the voice of the man who was on his walk. He called out, *Roger Hunt! Roger Hunt!*

It was John! The man I did not recognize was in fact my friend John Flagstaff! When I approached him, I could barely recognize that he was the man I knew so well. John was surprised and even ecstatic to see me. On the other hand, I was shocked because I still barely recognized him. He no longer had hair on any part of his head. He had no eyebrows. Parts of his eyelids were badly burned, and his ears were at least 50 percent destroyed.

I was horrified and could barely speak. I couldn't find any words to comfort John because I was looking only upon his outward appearance. I was surprised that he did not seem down or depressed. Essentially, I'd prejudged how I thought he should be acting and what he should be feeling.

I felt awkward that John had a more optimistic disposition than I had. He was actually trying to cheer me up. Here I was feeling sorry for John, but he was not in any kind of feeling-sorry-for-himself mood. With a smile on his scorched face, he was making it clear that he was grateful to be alive and grateful for my visit.

I learned much from visiting John that day. Primarily, I gained the perspective that I have nothing to complain about. I have no problems compared to his trials. I have no significant worries, and I have much to be grateful for. On that day, John was *turned-out* and I was a little *turned-in*.

Bradly Whitaker
Bradly is a quadriplegic. At the young age of seventeen, while hunting in the mountains, he fell headfirst from a tree about fifteen feet from the ground, breaking his neck and severing his spinal cord. Following his terrible accident, and with the sudden reality of his debilitating paralysis, Bradly received great support from his family, friends, and fellow church members. Through the years, Bradly learned to be positive and focused on succeeding in life. He received a college education in computer science and earned a high-tech engineering job with a major software company.

Currently, at the age of thirty, Bradly lives in beautiful house by himself and is largely independent, with some help from health-care professionals. He drives a van with specialized electronic features tailored to his needs.

Bradly is a contributing member of society in so many ways because he has learned to take advantage of all the resources available to him. He has also learned to be social and *turned-out* toward others in many ways, including being actively involved in helping and teaching paralyzed youth how to function and move their lives forward despite their disabilities. Bradly gets down and even gets depressed from time to time with the realization that he probably will never marry and have children, but he stays positive and active in his life. Instead of allowing himself to stay depressed, he serves as a lay minister for the Sunday school at his local church. He finds purpose in his life by teaching others to help themselves, and he experiences joy in many ways by being *turned- out*. He is a contributor, a builder of souls, and an inspiring example.

Edward Green
Ed Green was a young marine who was in the barracks in Beirut, Lebanon, in 1983 when terrorists bombed the facility. As a result of the terrorist attack, he was blown out of the building and pulverized by shrapnel, glass, and other debris. His body was torn and his bones were broken as he fell to the hard pavement below. He survived that ordeal, eventually earned a mechanical engineering degree, and then volunteered and fought valiantly in the First Gulf War in 1990, helping to free the people of Kuwait. There he suffered many other injuries, and afterward he endured the pains and horror of posttraumatic stress disorder. Later, he survived a rare but treatable form of pancreatic cancer. Ed was a fighter through those wars and his other challenges.

Throughout the years, Ed has been *turned-out* to others as a teacher and a successful consultant. Within the last three years, he lost both of his parents. He kept moving forward when he could have *turned-in* toward himself as a result of any of these ordeals; he could have chosen to feel sorry for himself, play the victim card, and accomplish nothing. Instead, Ed's mind-set is turned outward to work hard to achieve success as he serves others in his church and community.

Roger understood that all of these men had many challenges in their lives that were physically and emotionally debilitating, but instead of being *turned-in* to themselves, playing the victim card, staying discouraged, or allowing these difficult challenges to define them, they chose to be *turned-out* and serve others.

After a moment of reverent reflection of the experiences Roger had had with these three great men, he continued reading the BHIII memoirs with a grin of admiration.

Being Turned-In vs. Being Turned-Out

The following charts illustrate the different characteristics and results of individuals who are *turned-in* versus those who are *turned-out*. The first chart shows the characteristics that result from having either a *turned-in* mind-set or a *turned-out* mind-set. The second chart shows the earthly (temporal) and the eternal results of the two different mind-sets, based on the characteristics that come out of each mind-set.

Turned-In vs. *Turned-Out* Characteristics	
Turned-in **Mind-set**	*Turned-out* **Mind-set**
Self-serving	Serving others
Prideful	Humble
Selfish	Selfless
Dependent	Interdependent
Self-aggrandizing	Self-aware
Ungrateful	Full of gratitude

Temporal and Eternal Results of *Turned-In* and *Turned-Out* Mind-Sets	
Turned-in mind-set	*Turned-out* mind-set
Concerned with frivolous and vain things	Concerned with exalting things
Leads to fewer good friends	Cultivates lasting quality friendships
Leads to less freedom	Leads to more freedom

Leads to permanent failure	Leads to permanent success
Loses all in the end	Gains all eventually
Gains die with you	Gains rise with you

Being *turned-in,* you selfishly hold on to things and habits that will limit your growth or destroy you. If you really think about it, Roger, your gambling addiction probably started with one or more *turned-in* habits, which developed gradually and then nearly destroyed you.

Conversely, in being turned-out, Roger, you experience growth by caring for and serving those you love, including family and neighbors. Furthermore, in being turned-out, you learn to let go of self-defeating attitudes and selfish, debilitating habits that can lead to destructive addictions.

Why is this the case, Roger? Well, it's because when you get out into the real world and serve others freely, you find that you have fewer problems than what you first thought, compared to others. You become more grateful for what you have, and you tend to minimize how much you exaggerate your problems relative to others.

When you serve others and make a difference in their lives, you naturally grow, progress, and become a better person. Thus, you have less of a desire to make yourself feel better by way of artificial stimulation, using alcohol, using drugs, and engaging in other addictive behaviors.

Learning to be *turned-out* over the last few years, Roger, has saved you from returning to gambling, despite several temptations to go back to the casinos in the last thirteen years.

When we are *turned-in* and start forming bad habits and addictive behaviors, we tend to become ensnared in traps that result in less freedom, because that is where addictive behaviors lead, to less and less self-control and the ability to possess self-determination. The addiction will control you and rule over you. I have always enjoyed the analogy of the monkey trap as follows, which will help you better understand this principle:

The Monkey Trap

The South Indian monkey trap was developed by villagers to catch the ubiquitous small monkeys in that part of the world. The trap consists of a hollowed-out coconut attached to a stake. Inside the coconut is some rice, peanuts, or other treats that can be smelled and seen through a small hole. The hole is just large enough for the monkey to put its hand into it and grab a treat or two, but too small for its fist to emerge from after it grabs the prize.

Because of its greed for the prize, the monkey reaches in and grabs the goodies and then is suddenly trapped. The creature is not able to conceive that it is its own fist and the fistful of goodies that trap it, so insatiable is its desire for the loot. The monkey cannot let go, and by doing so it restrains its own freedom. So the trap works, and the villagers capture the unwitting creature.

Many of us in life lust after physical possessions and things that lead to bad habits. Roger, you know you have been caught in proverbial monkey traps before. You know firsthand how these traps can seduce you into believing that you can be successful if only you obtain vain possessions. Some of the habits that you have fallen into have led to addictive behaviors that have almost destroyed your goals and your pursuit of happiness and joy.

The process of adopting *turned- out* mind-sets will help you simultaneously adopt behaviors that give you courage and power to let go of the destructive things that limit your growth, in favor of reaching out and serving others.

Once there was a wise person who devised an important concept. *If you will elevate others, the very work itself will exalt you. Upon no other plan can a man justly or permanently aggrandize himself.*

Emphasize the Positive and Minimize the Negative MSA

Roger, conduct an MSE on your negative vs. positive mental attitude. As part of this exercise, ask yourself, *How often do I emphasize the negative aspects of my life? Do I often complain that I don't feel well? Do I murmur that I don't have as much money or as many physical possessions as my neighbor?*

If your negative thoughts and feelings outweigh your positive thoughts and feelings, maybe it is time for an MSA to emphasize more of the positive things in your life. Maybe it's time for you to consciously strive to de-emphasize the negative thoughts and feelings and strive to replace them with positive thoughts and feelings. There are two critical attitudes that are pivotal to this process: *gratitude and humility*. These two attitudes need to be focused upon and practiced on an ongoing basis. Make the following pledges with respect to gratitude and humility.

Gratitude

I pledge that I will strive to become a vessel of *gratitude* every day of my life. The process of becoming a vessel of *gratitude* helps me emphasize the positive things about me and the good things around me and helps me to be *turned-out* to serve others. There is a positive side to everything in life, especially in the trials and tribulations of life. The person who seeks to find the positive lessons, even during the failures and the disappointments of life, will develop the tools of courage and will engender the strength sufficient to overcome all of life's challenges.

Humility

I pledge to study and better understand the virtue of *humility. Humility* is the antithesis of the curse of pride. Where there is pride, there is a false sense of self-sufficiency to solve all things by the power of the natural man or woman. Proud people are stiff-necked, hard-hearted, and callous. The prideful are unable to sense the spiritual side of themselves. Humble people are teachable and full of faith—not only in themselves but also in others and in God. Humble people learn lessons from their failures and, in a contrite manner, learn to use their innate wisdom, their God-given talents, and the talents of others. They strive to draw upon the powers of heaven in a synergistic manner to solve their problems and overcome their weaknesses. *Humility*, or meekness as it is sometimes called, isn't to be confused with weakness. Jesus once said, *I am meek and lowly in heart* (Matthew 11:29), but he at the same time is the creator of all and is almighty, omnipotent, all-seeing, and all-knowing. So with help from the Divine, the humble man or woman will find infinite strength to conquer life's battles.

Roger, do you think it is possible that the reason you have not been as successful as you have desired to be may have something to do with your being *turned-in* more than being *turned-out*?

Are you neglecting opportunities to develop qualities of *humility, gratitude, and self-determination* in establishing success-oriented goals?

Do you think the fact that you developed a gambling addiction, which has many times derailed you from achieving and maintaining success, had anything to do with your lacking *turned-out* qualities? Like many others, you have pursued paths that are, at best, irrelevant and antithetical to maintaining success and, at worst, destructive to self and family. These destructive mind-sets and the paths they establish are the main reasons for otherwise preventable failures—even permanent failures if not corrected.

Self-absorbed and *turned-in* mind-sets can and will lead to destructive addictions, including drug or alcohol addictions; excessive food intake; shopping abuse; unchecked sexual behaviors, including pornography; and gambling—and other deleterious behaviors that can afflict and degrade each of the five components of the human soul. Our bodies and our souls become addicted to substances and behaviors; therefore, to overcome bad habits and addictions, our bodies and our souls need to unlearn the bad habits and addictions by employing the strongest measures necessary to free ourselves from them and replace them with good habits and constructive behaviors.

The following steps are designed to help people identify how they get into trouble with bad habits and addictions and how they can conscientiously keep themselves focused on the relevant good things (such as positive and transcending mind-sets and positive goals) that are needed to free them from the deleterious and negative things of this world.

Learning to Overcome Substance Use and Behaviors That Destroy the Human Soul: Introduction to Steps A through E

Roger, when you teach yourself negative mind-sets based on *turned- in* behaviors, you start to lose perspective, because in that selfish state all you think about is how to please and satisfy a fallacious perception of needs.

It is simply this: do we want good things or bad things in our lives? The choice is ours to either find the determination to replace the bad things with the good or not. It really is that simple.

Because there is so much misinformation in the world to the contrary of the obvious, there is ultimately a vast amount of confusion regarding which paths lead to success and which lead to mediocrity and failure. We live in a world that is becoming more and more *turned-in* to the self and that is; therefore, becoming more and more insensitive and callous to dangerous substances and behaviors. This insensitivity, confusion, and misinformation enables the unwitting and unwise to wander down destructive paths that lead to addiction, failure, and eventual destruction of a person's life.

In the same vein, the more *turned-in* you are, the more you choose paths of bad habits and addictions that turn you into your selfish-self, even more and more on a path toward your own self-destruction.

Also, genetically, some people, whether it is seemingly fair or not, may possess a greater inherent tendency to substance dependency and addiction. It is all part of living in a world that is naturally dominated by entropy. It might be said that the entropies of this world may affect each of us differently, at varying rates, and at various degrees of severity. Nevertheless, letting entropy get the best of us is ultimately no excuse. Because we are all children of God, each of us has the divine gift of agency, abilities, and talents to counteract and nullify the negative effects of entropy. The more we turn to God for answers, the more these divine gifts can provide us with sufficient power to help lift us above the natural man or woman.

Because we were born to win, we have innate abilities to proactively turn the tide on entropy and engulf our lives in positive behaviors that strengthen our souls, particularly as we strengthen others around us by learning to be *turned-out*.

Bad habits start to form, and before too long addictions set in as we embrace and actually bond with negative substances and behaviors. The negative effects of addictive substances and behaviors erode and destroy each of the five components of the human soul. The physical, spiritual, emotional, mental, and social sides to the human soul are degraded with the constant bombardment and abuse of illicit drugs, the use of tobacco in any form, and the overuse of alcohol. These things will first beat us up spiritually because these are antithetical to the core of spirituality.

Very soon we will find that these negative substances take a toll on us physically and emotionally as well. The normal functions of the human body simply cannot tolerate illicit drugs, tobacco, and excessive alcohol.

Roger, please do not confuse my aforementioned admonitions against these behaviors and substances to mean that I am judgmental of anyone or self-righteous. Nor should my sharing of these truths give you the impression that any person who falls into these habits and addictions (that I have chosen to call *bad*) should be judged or thought of as any less of a person or somehow should be ridiculed or shamed.

That is not the intent here, nor would that path be constructive or helpful. I am no judge, nor am I an example or model of anything close to perfection in any of these areas. But I strive to see things as they really are and to communicate the truth as it is established in order to help others who struggle. Do we not all struggle with something? Do we not each need help in some way or another?

Therefore, since many of us often fall into some form of bad habit or addiction, we need to know where we are at all times with respect to the behavior so we know when and how we can pull back and overcome the temptation to indulge in it.

Think of helping yourself combat negative habits and addictions by understanding and proactively disrupting what I have termed the **A–E steps** toward falling into the indulgences of destruction. The way I see it, if we go through steps A–D, defined below, without conscientiously disrupting that process, then by the time we are at E, it is *too easy* for us to fall into the habit or addiction—so we do.

Therefore, just as in the English alphabet, it all begins at A.

A. A Thought

It is totally natural to have thoughts, memories, or recollections of your bad habits and addictions. It will happen, especially if you have become addicted to some behavior or substance; you have bonded (to some degree or other) with that thing. So the memories of all the seemingly good things that you associate with the addiction will often pop into your mind, maybe triggered by a smell, feeling, or sight that reminds you of all or part of what was associated with the activities related to the addiction. You can be going in the right direction and on the right path one moment, and suddenly and without warning, there it is! It gets back into your mind. This is the point at which, if you can learn a process, system, or method to *exit out* by playing your exit card, you will have the greatest success in overcoming your habit or addiction. To succeed, you will need to learn a system to disrupt the process from A (a simple thought of the habit or addiction) to E (the point at which it is probably too difficult for you to *exit out* and avoid your habit or addiction, so you will easily fall into trouble). Your exit card has to be a conscious effort to replace the thought with either thinking or doing something else with a *louder volume* than the thought of the habit or addiction. The exiting-out process or playing the exit card could be something as simple as thinking of a favorite song, poem, or Parable of Jesus. It could also be some form of positive action, including an act of service. This interjection needs to be something positive that disrupts the bad thought before that bad thought starts to become appealing to you.

You may even need to call someone whom you can confide in and totally trust, someone you may even call your coach or your mentor. Be cautious with this method and choose your coach or mentor wisely. This person needs to be totally on your side and 100 percent invested in your well-being and happiness. He or she needs to be nonjudgmental and totally confidential when necessary, with the only exception being when additional or more-professional help is needed. All of this needs to be a planned system and not a haphazard or random method of giving you the help you need.

B. You Begin to Want It

If you do not exit out at step A, then you will soon begin to want and crave the substance, and as you continue forward, you will surrender to the addictive behavior. You begin to want it because you entertained the thought and associated it with the so-called pleasure or thrill that has become so much a part of you because you and embraced and even bonded with your addictions.

With a drug addiction, you remember the ecstasy of the high and being with friends who are also high until you live it mentally and desire it physically. When you are addicted to alcohol, you have very similar experiences and cravings associated with entertaining the thoughts and having the desire to participate in that addictive behavior. If you are a gambler and you spend too much time entertaining the thought of being adjacent to your favorite slot machine, in the poker room, or at the blackjack table, you will soon crave the thrill of a rare jackpot or the excitement of doubling down on a bet and getting lucky with a needed face card. You forget that the craving will eventually result in your enslavement.

Even being at the point of craving, you still have time and space to play your saving exit card; you can quickly extinguish your cravings by redirecting your thoughts and getting involved in something else, something positive and meaningful and aligned with your transcending goals.

Turn down the volume dial for your cravings by turning up your volume dial for the positive and constructive side. Redirect the bad and replace it with something good. Again, it is not too late to contact your confidant and mentor.

C. Consider and Conceive a Plan

You are at the point at which you start wanting the addiction back into your life, you mentally entertain the negative behavior, and you lean in the direction of bowing to your addiction. You then start considering and conceiving a plan to participate in the addictive behavior. As part of your planning, you begin to find out where and how to get your drugs and how to obtain the money to pay for them. You start thinking of getting money out of already depleted bank accounts, and you start contacting old friends and dealers who have sold you these substances previously. You may have even formulated a plan to steal from others in order to acquire the funds to buy the drugs or to gamble, further complicating your addictions with additional crimes. You still can and should find a way to replace this destructive plan with a new plan to get yourself out of trouble.

D. You Take the Detour

When you begin executing your plan, you are actually taking the detour and the path to participate. Because you begin executing your plan by getting the money and finding the casino, the liquor store, or the drug dealer, you then find yourself physically going there to participate in the addictive behaviors. But because you have not yet gotten the drugs or entered into the casino, you can still pull back, play your exit card, and bow out—but only with the highest level of effort. If you have obtained the money dishonestly, you will have to make restitution and pay the consequences consistent with your misdeeds. If you do not pull back immediately, you will fall off the wagon, because you have made it easy for yourself to participate.

E. Easy

Because you have not pulled back by playing your exit card, as you move deeply into step D, it is easy to fall back into your addictions.

Play your exit card before you get to E; the closer to step A, the greater the hope for success to stay free and/or clean. The sooner you play your exit card after A (a thought), the greater the chance you have in succeeding to overcome your addictive behaviors.

Learning to be *turned-out* and to serve others will give you meaning, power, and purpose to help you stay away from addictive behaviors or help you get out of addictive behaviors.

At 0800, by the end of Roger's morning readings and breakfast, it became obvious to him that the weather outside the Haynes cabin was beginning to worsen. A light rain was falling and appeared to be increasing with each passing moment. With this realization, Roger knew that the planned field labors of this day would not be easy. He knew he had to hike about five to six miles through wet, cold, and muddy conditions and monitor potential radiological hazards along the road in the area of the rare earth metals, along the northeast flanks of Bokan Mountain. Without haste or any further delay, by 0825 Roger quickly donned his rain gear and day pack and headed directly up the path and along the mining roads for the BHIII Vein area to complete the planned radiological monitoring for the day.

Due to rainy and muddy conditions, it took Roger about three and a half hours to climb and hike uphill to reach the BHIII Vein. Then it took about two hours to complete his monitoring activities. The results showed minimal elevated radiological impact to the mining roads in the rare earth deposit areas, which would be good news for Tyler and Selos once Roger completed his final reporting. It then took him about three hours to return to the Haynes cabin back at the marina. It had been a total of eight and a half hours of frustrating, wet, and muddy hiking conditions and monitoring up and down the slopes of Bokan Mountain.

Back at the Haynes cabin at 1700, Roger started a fire in the fireplace to warm himself and dry off his rain gear. He then prepared his dinner. *Ah! Freeze-dried beef stroganoff—one of my favorites,* Roger said to himself.

He then began preparing for the last three days, which would include hiking eight to nine miles to the Tyler cabin and heliport, located along the northwest flanks of Bokan Mountain, and to the northeast of Precipice Lake to conduct more radiological monitoring in that area. There Roger would finish up his work. Then Tyler and Selos would pick him up in the *Thunder Chicken* on Tuesday morning.

Roger knew that he needed a good restful sleep that night in order to make the arduous hike to the Tyler cabin in one day. He also knew that it would continue to get colder and colder with each passing night. As he checked the trending barometric conditions from the Haynes cabin's metrological station, Roger confirmed that tonight, with clearing skies, temperatures would be dipping down into the upper thirties, probably thirty-eight to thirty-nine degrees Fahrenheit. He also saw that there was an 80 percent chance of a cold rain overnight continuing throughout the morning. In preparation for a cold night, Roger put another log on the fire and allowed it to burn itself out as he slept.

With the fire burning brightly just ten feet from the foot of his bed and with his warm LA Dodgers quilt, Roger curled up for the night. At 2005, he fell into a slumber that would prove to produce some wondrous and fascinating dreams.

CHAPTER 10

MIND-SET 5: IMPROVE YOUR PERSONAL WEATHER FORECAST

Saturday, September 30 (Expedition - Day 6): The Yellow Key Card

As the night drew on, Roger began dreaming that he was on a small rickety fishing boat far offshore in an unknown body of water during a violent night time thunderstorm. The night was pitch-black, the moon and the stars veiled by the thick cloud cover from the raging storm. The only light available that enabled Roger to see the boat, its crew of twelve, and the conditions around him was from the nearly continual strikes of lightning in a 360-degree panoramic view around the vessel. He instantly understood he was a stowaway on the boat since he felt strangely out of time and out of place. The men on the boat were vigorously laboring to keep the vessel afloat as it pitched, rolled, and tossed about, nested in a body of mountain-sized waves.

With the waves continually breaking over the bow and across the port and starboard sides of the boat, water consistently hit Roger's face. He could taste the cool and rank-smelling waters as if he was really there as part of the crew. He deduced that he was on a body of freshwater rather than out to sea, based on the non-salty taste of the water.

Roger did not recognize any of crew. They were coarsely dressed in what appeared to be rags and robes with dull and dingy colors, probably from an ancient date, whereas he was dressed in his usual early twenty-first-century field garb, consisting of a North Face brand raincoat and Under Armour pants. Several of the crew hastily passed by in close proximity to Roger several times over a span of about fifteen to twenty minutes, bailing water out of the hull and working the vessel with their oars and rudder. They did not seem to notice that he was among them; he was apparently invisible to their view.

The panic in their eyes was real. The feeling was that of an exasperated and fatigued crew who were quickly reaching the end of their collective rope. At one point, out of desperation, several of the crew frantically began calling out in a language that sounded like Hebrew or Arabic. Their pleadings were directed to someone who was unseen. At first, Roger thought they were calling out to him, since they were facing him and yelling in his general direction. But then suddenly he noticed another crew member on the deck near the stern of the boat, just a few feet away from him, rising slowly from under a thick blanket, having been resting upon an old cushion or pillow. The crew seemed to be begging and pleading with their thirteenth member in the most urgent manner, questioning his apparent indifference to their survival.

As the new man stood, his demeanor seemed strong and calm, as if he were a mighty master and commander among common men. Roger witnessed that this man of majesty began to speak with power and authority to his acolytes. And as he did so, they immediately felt the comfort and gentle rebuke of his counsel.

Although Roger was not familiar with the master's language, he was able to understand the main message, which was that the disciples were to cease fearing and to believe and trust in what he was about to do.

At that moment, the master stretched his arms out into the air as if he were commanding the elements and the storm to obey him. The loud and authoritative command was mentally interpreted by Roger to mean, *Peace, be still*!

Miraculously, the storm was immediately abated. The gusty winds, the breaking waves, and the drenching rains that seconds ago had threatened to sink their vessel were gone. It was as if those things had never been present. Likewise, the rolling thunder and lightning strikes, along with the clouds from which they emanated, immediately dissipated, allowing a quarter moon and an accompanying array of bright stars to adorn the night.

Dead silence prevailed for seconds or even minutes. The servants began to gather and show a strange combination of amazement and fear. They began murmuring and reasoning with one another using fearful tones and expressions of befuddlement and shock. Judging by the puzzled look on their faces, the shaking of their heads, and their hand gestures, they seemed to be saying things such as, *How can this be?* and *How did he do it?* Roger was soon able to mysteriously decipher their talk and understood that they were also saying things like, *What kind of person is this among us who could perform such an immediate and decisive act?* and *The storm heard his commands and obeyed!* Roger could scarcely discern whether their new fear of such a man rivaled their fears of the actual storm itself.

In reality, this was only a dream, but as a silent third-party witness to an ethereal and ancient event, Roger was given a special gift of intellectual, emotional, and spiritual discernment at that moment. He was aware of a deeper meaning of an actual New Testament story, a meaning that was previously unknown to him or anyone else he knew. Roger found himself in a momentary state of suspended animation, separate from the dream as it were, which allowed him to experience a period of mediation and personal reflection.

A moment later, his dream resumed. Roger telepathically witnessed the Master discerning and considering the disciples' murmurings. He then confronted them, asking why they remained fearful, despite their having been delivered. He also asked them where their faith was and why it was so lacking during and even after the storm. Essentially, he said that their faith was trumped by fear, before and after their deliverance.

Roger also discerned that the Mater's words may have had even deeper meanings. Not only was the Master questioning their lack of collective faith in him, but also he was criticizing their lack of faith in the power within them. What if these novice disciples had the faith to take the initiative and perform the same miracle for themselves? Maybe the loving chastisement from the Master was a learning experience and a reminder that they too could have stepped forward with sufficient faith to rebuke the storm.

Roger was immediately edified in the understanding that had the disciples only resolved to overcome their fear with faith and exercised that faith by believing and then praying for deliverance and the heavenly powers above, they could have calmed the storm in the same manner. O how pleased their Master would have been with them at that moment. Nevertheless, Roger also understood that they needed the chastisement as part of an important lessons-learned moment. They needed to replace their fear with faith and action. Maybe these same disciples would remember this experience and know that they too had the Master's powers within them to help others in the future, even struggling individuals who also may be lacking in faith.

Upon gaining a new paradigm, Roger also acknowledged that the Master who had calmed the sea was indeed the very person known as Jesus of Nazareth, Roger's Lord and Savior.

At this point in the dream, Roger's Lord turned to him, and in a smiling and loving manner telepathically communicated the following message: *Roger, you have experienced many emotional and spiritual storms in your life that should have humbled you and brought you to your knees. You know that you have my power within you to command, 'Peace, be still.' You need to learn to not fear, but to have the faith and resolve to calm your own emotional and spiritual storms before your anger destroys you and your loving relationships.*

These words, and the loving manner in which they were communicated, melted Roger's heart. He felt a burning within his soul that rivaled all his previous spiritual experiences up to that point in his life. He knew this message was a divine gift. It was a kind but stern admonition for him to get his personal and emotional life in order and to learn that he could calm his own emotional storms, just as the Master himself had once calmed a temporal storm.

Then, in conclusion, the Master pointed to the infinite body of water behind Roger, as if to call his attention to something of interest. When Roger turned his head to observe the object, he immediately noticed that it was the familiar glowing figurine. It was the Magnificent Mind-Set Man, which quickly moved in his direction and then suddenly stopped a few feet in front of him. One of the puzzle pieces flashed brightly, exhibiting the acronym PBS and then turning yellow. Roger immediately remembered from his experience in the underground mine that this meant, *Peace, be still.*

Roger abruptly awoke and found himself in his bed in the Haynes cabin. The clock read 0615. Having all the details of the dream firmly embedded in mind, Roger immediately located the yellow key card on the dining room table and used it to open the safe. The contents included a new figurine and additional pages in the binder.

The new figurine was of a man's hand firmly grasping a single bolt of lightning striking near him, as if to portray the concept of gaining control over one's own personal and violent emotional or mental storms.

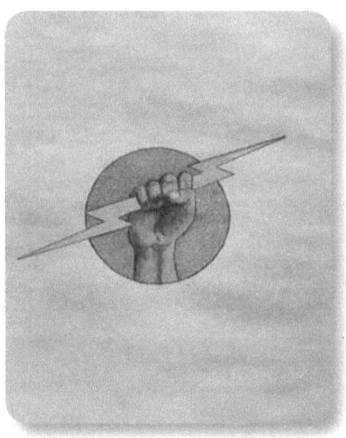

Roger eagerly began reading the new pages of text.

Improve Your Personal Weather Forecast: Learn to Command, *Peace, Be Still*

Having PMA and possessing a happy continence will greatly enhance your life and your relationships with others. Learn to have attitudes of gratitude and appreciation every day of your life, Roger. Ponder and focus on the analogy presented below.

My Personal Weather Forecast MSA

How is your personal weather forecast, Roger? And why is this an important question?

Well, Roger, it's important because how you think and feel is often how you react to stress, conflict, and challenges.

So, Roger, I ask you again to think about this question: how is your personal weather forecast? How do you feel about and respond to life's daily stressful and challenging situations?

Ask yourself these questions: Does stress or unrest cause personal storms of sorrow, anger, and contention? Do you experience clouds or foggy horizons of depression? Are you overcome with lightning storms of frustration, and do you lose control from time to time? Or is your personal weather forecast dominated by fair to partly cloudy or sunny and mild conditions, because you have learned to calm your proverbial storms and the rough seas that could threaten your mental well-being and your life?

Roger, you have the power to establish your own personal and emotional weather patterns that form around you. It is up to you to evaluate (conduct an MSE) and adjust your mind-set (conduct an MSA) to allow yourself the benefit of a sunny pathway forward in life, despite the challenges, setbacks, or adversities that you experience in life.

Your personal weather pattern is established by how you react to the various fluctuating negative and positive stimuli that affect you during your life. You can choose to be happy, optimistic, and proactive regardless of the negative things you experience. The positive attitudes establish a sunny emotional weather pattern around you. This gives you power to see *in the light,* because you are living in the light of wisdom and love. Thus your vision is clear, full of light, full of self-control, and full of self-direction.

You can also choose to react in negative ways during your trials. You can choose to let things get you down (rain showers, fog); you can choose to feel depressed and stay depressed (constant dark and dreary rain showers and storms). In such a circumstance, you cannot see as well, because the dark clouds, the heavy rains, and the fog distort your view of life. However, if you are depressed because of chemical imbalances, you may not have the power to simply choose not to be depressed, but you can choose to get professional and even medical help to be treated for such aliments.

You can also choose to get angry. You can take out your frustrations on yourself and others to cope with adversity. Such retaliations can come out in the form of verbal or physical abuse or both.

Also, during your dark displays of anger, you might break things, get road rage, or lash out in frustration at family and friends. The last of these three reactions destroys relationships, hurts others, and can possibly cost you your freedom, as you could end up in jail or prison if you choose to hurt others.

Ask yourself, Roger, *What is my current personal weather pattern? How do I react to negative situations, stress, and anger toward others?* Or, looking into the future, and based on what you want to establish for yourself, *What is my personal weather forecast going to be like tomorrow?* You have the gift of agency and other divine gifts; therefore, you can choose your own forecast and find the power within you to change your personal weather pattern from negative to positive.

The Savior calmed the winds and the waves on the tempestuous Sea of Galilee by saying, *Peace, be still*! And his disciples asked in shock and awe, *What manner of man is this?*

The Savior may be the only one in earth's history who had and used this kind of power over the earthly elements in a manner sufficient to change the physical and regional weather in an instant. But in a metaphorical sense, my argument to you, Roger, is that you have the power to change your own personal weather forecast through focus, self-will, and self-control. You can say to yourself in any situation, *Peace, be still. Be calm!* You can do it, too!

Remember the lyrics of the following song:

Master, the Tempest Is Raging
By Mary Ann Baker and H. R. Palmer

Master, the tempest is raging!
The billows are tossing high!
The sky is o'ershadowed with blackness.
No shelter or help is nigh.
Carest thou not that we perish?
How canst thou lie asleep?
When each moment so madly is threat'ning
A grave in the angry deep?

Master, with anguish of spirit
I bow in my grief today.
The depths of my sad heart are troubled.
Oh, waken and save, I pray!
Torrents of sin and of anguish
Sweep o'er my sinking soul,
And I perish! I perish! dear Master.
Oh, hasten and take control!

Master the terror is over.
The element sweetly rest.
Earth's sun in the calm lake is mirrored,
And heaven's within my breast.
Linger, O blessed Redeemer!
Leave me alone no more,
And with joy I shall make the blest harbor
And rest on the blissful shore.

The winds and the waves shall obey thy will:
Peace, be still.
Whether the wrath of the storm-tossed sea
Or demons or men or whatever it be,
No waters can swallow the ship where lies
The Master of ocean and earth and skies.
They all shall sweetly obey thy will:
Peace, be still; peace, be still.
They all shall sweetly obey thy will:
Peace, peace, be still.

As Roger read these new pages, he remembered a personal experience during the fall of 2002 that he had often thought about and reflected upon throughout the years.

Roger opened up his journal and started writing about the past experience. He suggested to himself a plan of personal application to help him improve his personal weather forecast, thus tying together his past experience and today's lessons from Billy's writings.

It's Wherever You Want It to Be

During a family vacation with my four children approximately eleven years ago, while on the island of Oahu and near Waikiki Beach, I was walking a path lined with a group of large banyan trees that eventually led to a series of shops and souvenir booths. I happened to enter an art gallery, where I started enjoying several paintings by talented local artists portraying beautiful tropical landscapes. Many of these, I concluded, had to be depictions of various famous places, some of which I wanted to visit while on the Hawaiian Islands. One painting in particular that caught my attention was of a beautiful waterfall setting adorned with lush vegetation and glorious rays of sunlight. The painting displayed so many of nature's colors, shades, and tropical designs that I just had to find this place to experience this wonder firsthand. So, I grabbed the store attendant's attention and asked the gentleman, *Where on this island can I find this paradise?*

The young man, appearing like a typical hippy from the 1970s, looked at me with his dreamy eyes as if to say, *What do you mean, where is this place?* When he remained silent, I repeated my question. Sir, where is this place? *I want to go there someday.*

He then gave me a silly look and replied, *It's wherever you want it to be.* Then he turned and walked away, leaving me speechless and pondering the meaning of his strange reply.

After a while, the meaning of the *it's wherever you what it to be* comment came to me. I concluded that maybe this painting was of a place that was nowhere in particular. Or maybe it was a variety of places all combined into one painting with the artist's favorite highlights from each place. Regardless, the point is simply this: There are many different places you have visited during your life, either physically or mentally. Each of these places has lifted and inspired you in unique ways and has left an image burned deep into your mind, one that you will never forget.

Whether real or imagined places, or combinations of real and imagined places, you can visit such paradises over and over again in your mind. You can use this methodology as a tool to comfort, soothe, and enlighten your mind and lift your spirit. You can *go there* mentally or spiritually at any time, during any circumstance, to help calm your storms or heal your broken heart. During times of stress, anxiety, or depression, you can *go there.*

Developing this ability to transition mentally, emotionally, and spiritually to a different and better place is, in a sense, a *peace, be still* moment. Such moments need to occur often in your life to help you improve your personal weather forecast and give you more emotional self-control.

Following his daily reading of Billy's writings and his personal journal entry, Roger soon came back to reality with a glance out the window of the Haynes cabin. He noticed that the rains continued to fall. His local weather forecast, according to the Haynes meteorological station, was showing winds holding steadily at fifteen miles per hour. Temperatures were currently in the low fifties but would start to fall to the mid-forties by midday, and the barometric pressure was also showing signs of falling. Roger didn't have to be a meteorologist to know that these readings indicated more foul weather ahead, which would likely prevail throughout the day and may even increase in intensity as the day wore on. *It looks like the annual severe October rains are returning early this year on Prince of Wales Island,* Roger concluded.

The forecast of bad weather, combined with the importance of staying on plan, weighed heavily upon Roger's mind. He knew he needed to get to the Tyler cabin on the northwest side of Bokan Mountain, near Precipice Lake, by nightfall, despite the weather. He also knew that he had only two and a half days of radiological readings left (Sunday, Monday, and Tuesday morning), which needed to take place around Precipice Lake before Tuesday's scheduled pickup time at the Tyler Cabin.

Therefore, Roger quickly finished breakfast and hastily gathered up all of his gear, his field equipment, and his .44 Magnum and loaded his pack. Because he needed to hike about ten miles in the rain that day, he needed to get going before 0800, so he quickly donned his rain gear and waterproof boots and left the Haynes cabin.

About a quarter of the way up the mining road, Roger suddenly remembered he would not be going back to the Haynes cabin. He wanted to quickly return to see if he could gather up the remaining key cards (the orange and red ones), the Magnificent Mind-Set Man figurine, each of the other five figurines, and the BHIII memoirs from the safe.

He felt that the figurines and writings were a gift from Billy and that Billy would expect him to take the writings and symbols, continue to learn from them, and share the ideas with others. After all, Billy had written everything directly to him.

However, upon returning to the Haynes cabin, Roger found, to his disappointment, that the safe was shut tight with all the symbols and Billy's writings locked inside. Only the two remaining key cards, the orange and the red, remained on the dining room table. Roger tried each card to see if either would open the safe, but neither would. *Dang it! I knew I should have packed them all up while I still could*, he complained.

Roger knew that he had left the safe open when he'd left the cabin earlier that morning. He decided that Billy must have visited the Haynes cabin in those few minutes and locked the items away. It must have been Billy's intention that Roger not actually possess these items. Instead, Roger needed to work from memory to write and speak about these new ideas, after first growing and improving his own life by practically applying the principles.

From Roger's standpoint, not finding the writings or the symbols was a major setback to his plans to potentially get rich with the figurines, writings, and ideas. But using the writings and symbols to get rich and famous was not Billy Haynes's intent in sharing them with Roger. Nor was it the purpose of his works and writings.

Roger left the cabin a little confused and somewhat discouraged. As he started on his way back up the trail to resume his hike for the day, he noted that there was a momentary hiatus of the falling rain, and even the dense cloud cover parted to give a ray or two of morning sunlight.

Roger stopped in his tracks and pondered a moment or two about this past week and all that he had been able to accomplish for his clients, as well as all the important new concepts that Billy Haynes had miraculously shared with him through the Magnificent Mind-Set Man and the other figurines and writings.

He also felt grateful that Billy mysteriously had been there to save him from dangerous circumstances a couple of times during his expeditions.

This really has been a special and unique week here at Bokan Mountain, Roger confessed under his breath as he resumed his trek to the Tyler cabin.

Before he got two or three strides up the path, Roger again heard the call of the wild from his patron eagle, which again gave him encouragement and enlightenment to remember all the important details of Billy's writings and the meanings of each of the symbolic figurines. He was also able to recall each of the wondrous dreams he had experienced that week and their meanings in relation to the Seven Transcending and Magnificent Mind-Sets of Success. Everything was remembered and stored in his mind in a single instant, thanks again to the majestic call of the wild.

This made Roger feel even more humbled and blessed by these gifts from Billy Haynes. In appreciation and joy, Roger yelled out loudly in the direction of Bokan Mountain, *Thank you, Billy*!

Strangely, Roger swore he heard words echoing back from the southern cliffs of his favorite mountain: *You're welcome*!

At this point, Roger was no longer surprised by the strangeness of these experiences or by any of the other phenomena he had witnessed on Bokan Mountain. Rather, he was getting used to the uncanny events.

Although Roger was strengthened and refreshed by these experiences, he knew he had no time to waste. He needed to get moving to make it to the Tyler cabin before nightfall. So in haste, he resumed his path forward along the mining road and up the hill around Bokan Mountain.

Meanwhile, in the Haynes cabin, a voice came over the ham radio. *Roger! Roger! Can you hear me? Roger?*

It was the voice of Eddie Tyler.

Again, the voice called out, *Roger! Roger, please come in, Roger! If you can hear me, Roger, please do not hike to the Tyler cabin today. We will pick you up on Tuesday around noon at the Haynes cabin. Just hunker down and stay where you are, Roger. You will be safe there until we get you on Tuesday. A dangerous low-pressure weather system is fast approaching toward the west side of Bokan Mountain. The storm will hit this afternoon, and it will be too dangerous for you to be hiking in that area today. Heavy rains will pound, and winds will reach up into the forty-five -mile- per-hour range. I repeat, Roger, do not travel to the Tyler cabin today. Stay at the Haynes cabin.*

This message was repeated three times, with no answer from Roger. It was too late for Roger to hear the message since he was well on his way to the Tyler cabin by then. Now he was left to face the wildlife and difficult trails on Bokan Mountain. He was also left to the mercy of the elements and inclement weather that lay ahead. But that day he was armed with his new-found optimism, enthusiasm, and purpose in life from the week's lessons. He also had the protection of his spirit guide, Billy Haynes, and his Magnificent Mind-Set Man, which would likely make the difference in his survival and success going forward.

CHAPTER 11

THE MOUNTAIN, THE WEATHER, AND THE MAGNIFICENT MIND-SET MAN

The first six miles of Roger's journey were easy enough. He began hoping he would reach the cabin on schedule. However, throughout the rest of the morning and into the early afternoon, the weather started producing a rare dense fog along the first mile and a half along the lower elevations of the mountain. The fog cleared to offer another brief glimmer of sunlight but then quickly gave way to increasing cloud cover, rain, and wind.

As the day drew on and the weather worsened, Roger started thinking about and pondering over his wondrous dream the night before and the messages and inspired writings about using *peace, be still* moments to gain emotional control. Those thoughts edified and strengthened him during the day. He began drawing analogies and comparisons to good and bad weather conditions and the feelings and emotions that he had experienced throughout his life when faced with each of the various emotional weather events.

Roger began evaluating his feelings and mind-sets during the different conditions; he noticed that earlier in the morning, when he had experienced a brief ray of sunlight, he had felt joy and happiness and found it easy to recall the positive things that had happened during the week. When he went through dark and foggy conditions, he felt somewhat dreary and a little depressed, this because of focusing more on the negative things that had occurred during that day and the expedition as a whole. Coming out of the fog into brief sunshine, and then back into darkening conditions of cloudiness, rain, and wind, produced mixed emotions of sadness, happiness, and then sadness again.

When a thunderstorm accompanied by hail abruptly hit him in the early afternoon, the trail got muddier and slipperier. As conditions became more difficult, Roger felt some anger and frustration. These conditions caused him to lose emotional control and to focus on his frustrated plan for the day. He even began to cuss and swear as he lost footing from time to time and began slipping off the trail a little here and there—even falling face-first a couple of times.

As he looked back on his life, Roger started to realize that even though he may not have control over the physical weather sometimes inflicted upon him, he did have the ability to control himself, keep his focus, and keep his emotional responses in check during difficult weather or other frustrating times in life. Remembering that stormy day in order to refocus and think about the *peace, be still* moments really did seem to help him control his emotions more effectively. To mentally and consciously regain control over his emotions, he did his best to go to those *beautiful places* in his mind to calm himself. He tried to refocus his thoughts on more positive mental pictures, calming music, and other such things. These exercises produced comforting emotions, which were needed that stormy day.

But at about 1615, as the light of the day lessened and the storm continued to strengthen, Roger realized that he would need a larger dose of this remedy, or maybe even some more help from his friend and spirit guide.

The winds increased to the twenty-five- to thirty-mile-an-hour range, the rain began falling in a nearly horizontal trajectory, and temperatures were dipping into the upper thirties.

These were some of the more dangerous stretches of the trail to the cabin, particularly during bad weather conditions. Steeper and rockier slopes rose to a final summit before gradually plunging into a thicker forest of trees, where the cabin lay, about a mile ahead. In his mind, Roger could almost feel the warmth of the fire he would build and the hot dinner he would prepare and taste within the next few minutes upon reaching the Tyler cabin. He would get there just before dark.

Oh, how good that will feel! he thought.

Then, with 0.9 miles to go before reaching the Tyler cabin on the northwestern slopes of Bokan Mountain, Roger was frightened and amazed to spot another black bear standing on the trail about 100 feet in front of him. *Is this Chloe or another bear that I have fortuitously come upon, and what is this beast doing out in this type of weather?*

These questions quickly became irrelevant when the bear suddenly turned and viewed Roger. She growled and snarled as if to say, *I've got you now, my tasty little friend, and this time there is no Billy Haynes around to bail you out!*

As quickly as he could, Roger threw off his pack, opened it, and pulled out his .44 Magnum. The bear began charging him. He noticed that his opened pack had dumped equipment out onto the wet and muddy ground, but he didn't think that was important at the time since he needed to get a series of shots fired off to stop this roaring bear in her tracks. Otherwise, he would be the bear's one-course dinner for the night.

After Roger shot once and then twice at the bear, he suddenly lost his footing and slipped down the side of the rocky and slippery trail, losing his gun and all his gear and equipment. He rolled and tumbled about thirty feet down the steep slope, coming to a sudden stop on a small ledge of slate at the edge of a ten-foot cliff, hovering above another cliff, which plunged another thirty or more feet below.

So there he was, alone, afraid, and wet, with bumps and bruises but no apparent broken bones. But he was still in danger. Fortunately, the winds and the rain began to slowly dissipate. As the night was drawing on and darkness was beginning to prevail, Roger looked up and thought he saw the dark figure of somebody or something standing above him. Was it the bear? Or was it his mind creating an illusion after a bad bump to his head because of the fall?

Then he heard a familiar voice calmly saying, *It looks like you're going to be okay again, Roger! You know, it's a good thing you missed Chloe and fell down there! I think she was really mad at you this time. I chased her away again, so you don't have to worry about her anymore tonight.*

Roger's mouth gaped wide open for several seconds in amazement that Billy Haynes was here again at the moment when he needed him the most. Before he could say a word or think another thought, he felt a three-quarter-inch-thick rope falling onto his head and then all around him. Then he heard Billy say, *Here you go, Roger! You remember how to tie a bowline from when you were in the Boy Scouts, I trust?*

Yeah, I know how! Roger replied.

Well, good on ya! So tie one around you, and I'll pull you up. Just give it a tug when you're ready, and then we'll get you up here in two shakes of a lamb's tail!

With the knot correctly tied and the rope placed firmly around his waist, Roger tugged as directed. He then felt a sudden tension applied to the rope, making it as taut as a guitar string. Within a couple of minutes, with relative ease, and with only a few slips and slides against the slick rock wall, Roger finally made it to the top of his little cliff. Before he could thank Billy, he noticed that the rope was firmly attached to the nearest fir tree with a perfect taut-line hitch, but there was no sign of the man who had helped him so expediently.

Roger called out, *Billy? Billy?*

But there was no reply.

By this time it was almost completely dark, but the rain and the winds had stopped. Roger quickly made his way back to the trail to find his pack and equipment so he could get to the Tyler cabin safely for the night, before something else could happen. Roger found most of his equipment and gear in good shape and unharmed, including his gun. But much to his chagrin, he noted that the scintillation counter was missing. Not only was this meter needed to finish his work over the next two days, but also the instrument electronically held all the data and data point locations from his earlier radiological readings. If he could not find the meter, at least half his work would be gone and half his investigative activities wasted; such a loss would be embarrassing and would potentially damage his relationship with his clients.

Just when Roger began to think that things couldn't get any worse, he wandered a little from the trail and lost his way in the dark. After several minutes of frantically looking around for the meter, using his less-than-effective flashlight, he realized that he was in trouble again. Without a quick and clear way of finding the trail to the Tyler cabin, Roger was in danger of developing hypothermia. With a wet, hurt, and fatigued body, he again started to panic.

But his panic was soon allayed with the sound of Billy calling out, *Follow the Mind-Set Man, Roger! Follow the Mind-Set Man!*

There, suddenly appearing fifty feet in front of him, was the illuminated Magnificent Mind-Set Man figurine. When Roger approach the figurine, it began to move in a direction that led him directly to the Tyler cabin.

Roger was happy, to say the least, to get to the cabin. And to his extreme pleasure and bewilderment, he found an unlocked door. Upon walking inside, he smelled the pleasant aroma of chicken stew and felt the warmth of a cozy fire in the wood-burning stove. Unfortunately, there was no sign of Billy, so Roger couldn't thank him.

Before bedtime, Roger felt all the mixed emotions of the day. He recalled the gift of the morning education and edification, the difficulties of the day resulting from extreme weather conditions, and being saved from the bear and the cliff but losing the scintillation counter. Nevertheless, the feeling of being safe, comfortable, and all in one piece seemed to eclipse the setbacks, the cuts and bruises, and the lost meter. He had a certain feeling of optimism and encouragement. He was convinced that if he refrained from pitying himself and refused to give up, in tomorrow's daylight he would find the lost meter and his expedition would be a success. He felt that everything would work out just fine in the end and he would be able to finish each of his planned tasks on the north side of Bokan Mountain by Tuesday.

In preparation for the next day, he spread out all his gear and equipment on the table next to the woodstove to dry. Included in the array of items were the orange and red key cards, which he knew still had a purpose and would be the means for him to receive more enlightenment over the next couple of days.

With his new sense of optimism, Roger soon made his way into a small but warm twin-sized bed, mysteriously equipped with another blue and white LA Dodgers quilt. Being totally exhausted, he fell fast asleep.

In a deep slumber, Roger was again blessed by dreams. But tonight, there was a series of dreams that took him back a few years, remembering his children at different times of their lives when they endured struggles and challenges. Some of their trials were typical and some were unique. Some were serious and others seemingly frivolous. But each taught Roger a lot about his children's character and their determination never to give up in life when faced with sometimes difficult challenges.

Roger remembered each of them and the sports they would play from the ages of eight through fifteen, such as little league baseball, softball, and soccer, as well as when they'd learned to ski, ride bicycles, and do other such things. He relived teaching them never to give up and to keep doing their best, despite their varying physical or athletic abilities.

His dreams then began to focus on each of his four children one by one.

When his mind reflected on his eldest son, Ricky, he remembered the joy of holding his first child in his arms and knowing what it was like to love someone more than he loved himself. Of course he also felt that same joy and deep sense of love while holding each of his other three children once they came into the world.

But he knew in his heart that Ricky had a special mission to fulfill on earth. Ricky grew up with a touch of autism; more specifically, he was diagnosed with a form of what professionals call Asperger syndrome. He experienced a high degree of excitement, anxiety, and sometimes ultra-enthusiasm in his social relationships with other children, but his condition also led to a high degree of intelligence in the areas of reading, mathematics, and analytical problem solving, which allowed him to excel in a number of ways in his educational pursuits throughout the years. He did have some struggles and a hard time adjusting to change, and he'd had to learn patience while his school caught on to his fast pace of learning. But because he always tried hard in social settings as well as academic settings, Ricky always had friends and was loved by all his schoolmates. Ricky became a skier, as did his younger siblings; he enjoyed karate more than more traditional sports such as baseball or soccer.

Ricky learned to deal with his social challenges and other struggles to the point that he was able to excel in high school and earn scholarships to college. He then successfully got accepted into medical school, and now he was in his second year of studies at the University of Utah.

With regard to his son Michael, Roger relived the difficulties the boy had with debilitating anxiety and depression. He also struggled in sports but still played hard, especially in baseball. He loved to ski, so he skied hard. He loved mathematics and was interested in engineering. Michael studied hard in college and graduated with honors with a degree in architectural design. He was now a very productive member of society, working for a large architectural firm in the San Francisco Bay Area. He also had a big heart and supported many charitable institutions and events, including Habitat for Humanity, and helped with fund-raising for a cure for AIDS. It would have been easy for Michael to have given up, but he kept moving his life forward in a positive manner, always in pursuit of worthy and aggressive goals that he believed in and worked toward.

Roger then had dreams of events in his two girls' lives. He even created and memorized poems about their young lives, recalling many cute memories but also the many trials and challenges they had endured.

For Allyson, Roger wrote the following in his heart and mind:

> When she was younger and just a small kid,
> She made friends with all; that's what she did.
> She was spunky and precocious; none did she deny.

She was natural and fun; on her charm she'd rely.
Her excitement one day was hard to contain.
Arriving at Disneyland, she was a happy young dame.
A gleeful face, a perpetual smile,
An ear-to-ear grin that lasted a while.
She loved all our trips; she loved to fish and hike.
She'd bait her own hook with worms: Oh yikes!
She has always loved *an-mos*; she says, *They're cool*.
Especially she loves all the *horsies*, dogs, and wolves.
At one time, thanks in large part to her kindness and heart,
We owned half the animals in our old neighborhood part.
We had three hamsters, a bunny, and several tiny frogs.
But that's not all, for we had two cats and one cute dog.

Who is that little girl way up in the tree?
It's my girl, it's my kid, it is only she!
I heard her sweet voice, and above me I saw
My four-year-old up a maple tree; I was in awe.
She got way up there, maybe twelve or more feet.
I thought she was in danger or in for a defeat.
But much to my comfort, she got down in a flash.
Then on to a new challenge, she was off in a dash.
I knew then she had the courage and the guts.
She'd climb any mount or drive her dad nuts.
I knew she could conquer all trials put in her way.
You could tell she was proactive, as she'd rule the day.
I am glad I was right.
I'm glad for the sight,
Because during her young life,
She would experience some strife,
But with great courage, on faith she would lean.
She would not give up; she was one tough teen.
And with support from family and friends—
With all our prayers—she endured to the end.
She survived the surgeries, the illness, and pain.

She had the perspective and knew she'd gain.
One day while skiing, we had a great scare.
My girl's coat got caught on a ski-lift chair.
As we unloaded, I skied off and went to the left,
But around she went, being dragged to near her death.
Her scream was loud and shrill;
I did not know what I could do.
But an alert operator stopped the rig.
She was safe, we all knew.
You'd think that was it, you'd think she was through,
But instead, she keeps skiing until in the face she's blue.
In softball she loved to play catcher and all the bases indeed.
In high school, she sang in the choir.
She enjoyed the whole thing.
She worked really hard, and her grades were top-notch.
She laid a firm foundation.
She'll succeed, just watch.
She has passion and desire; she has the will to win.
With determination and will, she'll bear trials and grin.

For Valarie, Roger wrote the following:

When she was one-point-two,
I felt a tug at my shoe.
I looked down to see
What it could be.
What I saw, it was so cute!
It was Val! It was Val,
In her Halloween devil suit!
She was red with sharp horns and a black pointy fork.
The costume was a hit, and she was full of kid torque.
With red-rose baby cheeks and a heart of desire,
She was ready to go out and set the world on fire.

When she was six or so, she wanted to master the bike.
She wanted to be as her older bros and sis, just like!
She wanted to race and ride.
With style she wanted to glide.
She said, *Dad! Just give me a push to get me started.*
Then down she went.
Crash! She was brokenhearted.
With bruises and scrapes, she didn't give up.
She wanted to conquer; she wanted to win.
And so she said, *Let's try it again!*
But this time, let's take it slow,
But not on the road, no, no, no!
Push me while I ride on the grass.
Let's try it this way.
Don't argue, don't sass!
And there she went, riding and gliding, first on the lawn,
Then to the sidewalk, to the road, all night long 'til dawn.
At age eight, she wanted to ski.
She loves the mountains; she loves the snow!
She wanted to conquer that one too, you know.
But when she tried,
She fell, she got bruised, and she cried.
Dad, I can't do this, I'll never catch on.
I'm just a failure. I feel like a moron.
But then I taught her this little jingle.
I said,
Stick to the task 'til it sticks to you ...
Bend at it, sweat at it, smile at it, too;
For out of the bend and the sweat and the smile
Will come life's victory after a while.
With this new thought, with this in mind,
She tried again with a new paradigm.
Well, persistence paid off as she learned a new thrill.
She's now a good skier, the queen of the hill.

When she was nine, during one of her soccer games,
She was playing her heart out with the rest of the dames.
Then she got hit square in the face!
Ouch, that hurt! Out of the game she came.
There on Dad's lap
Is where she sat.
Don't worry, my child, you won't get hit again.
Just think of it this way:
Lightning never strikes twice on my kid.
So she tried it again. She went back out onto the field,
And in a flash, it happened again!
Another kicked ball hit her in the head,
And she fell to the ground but was far from dead.
Again she came out,
But only with a pout.
Then while sitting on my lap, she was nearly
beaned by a ball that went foul.
With a chuckle, the ref yelled,
What is with you? and gave her a bow.
But despite it all, she went back into the game.
And again she was hit; yes, in the face she was hit.
Number three?
Three times in the same day.
You'd think she'd quit.
But she stayed in the game and didn't sit.
The fans, her team, her foes, gave her a cheer,
A standing ovation that lasted a year.
She was my heroine, and I'll never forget
Her courage to conquer, her fervor, her grit!

Both of Roger's girls had reasons to become discouraged in their early years, but they kept pushing forward with their ambitions and goals and, like their brothers, excelled in high school and college.

CHAPTER 12

MIND-SET 6: NEVER GIVE UP!

Sunday, October 1 (Expedition - Day 7):
The Orange Key Card

Roger awoke promptly at 0655, refreshed and invigorated. He was all smiles and happy tears, remembering and cherishing the many memorable experiences he'd had with his children through the years, from their childhood to maturity. As Roger arose from his bed, he immediately noted that the fire was still mysteriously burning in the woodstove and the Tyler cabin was still warm and cozy on that cold and wet Sunday morning. As he started preparing breakfast by boiling water on the flat surface of the woodstove for the freeze-dried scrambled eggs and sausage, he was surprised to note a new addition to the Tyler cabin. It was the same old black Liberty safe that he knew so well from the Haynes cabin, standing right between the woodstove to the left and the kitchen sink to the right.

Without haste, Roger approached the table, grabbed the orange key card, and used it to open the safe. Upon peering into the safe, he noted another metal figurine and a slightly thicker binder of Billy's writings, which included a new chapter.

The new figurine was a hand-sized model of two ski poles, a soccer ball, and a baseball bat, all welded together in one continuous piece, with a karate black belt holding the image together. Roger immediately knew that this new symbol stood for the concept of never giving up, the sports-related emblems indicative of the activities his children had persevered in, as well as the other personal challenges they had been able to overcome.

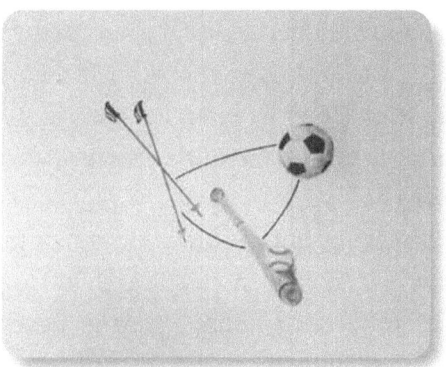

Roger then began reading the next chapter, as follows:

Mind-Set 6: Never Give Up! Stick to the Task!

Roger, establish a *never give up* attitude and have an insatiable desire to succeed. A *nothing will get in my way* attitude is needed to succeed in this fast-paced world of continual competition and stress. Your failures are only temporary setbacks and should be considered learning experiences, giving you important lessons in life and better tools to succeed.

Roger, please read and memorize this inspiring poem, written by an unknown author:

Stick to Your Task MSA

> Stick to your task 'til it sticks to you;
> Beginners are many, but enders are few.
> Honor, power, place, and praise
> Will come in time to the one who stays.

> Stick to your task 'til it sticks to you;
> Bend at it, sweat at it, and smile at it, too;
> For out of the bend and the sweat and the smile
> Will come life's victories after a while.

Each time you get frustrated or discouraged in life, and every time you seem to be overwhelmed with trials and setbacks, repeat this poem either in your mind or out loud. Repeat these phrases over and over, again and again, louder and louder each time. Each time you repeat this poem, do so with more and more meaning and enthusiasm, until you feel the truth and strength of its intended message. Teach this poem to others and encourage them to memorize these inspiring words and pass them along to others as well.

No doubt it is a cliché, but the phrase *If at first you don't succeed, try, try again* has a deeper and hidden meaning to it, Roger. Please consider the idea that this process of falling, getting back up, falling again, getting back up again, and so on and so forth is a learning process, a series of rehabilitating repetitions—even a form of mental, intellectual, and emotional exercise.

Just as a regimen of weight-lifting exercises strengthens one's muscles with various reps and sets, a regimen of falling, getting up, and try, trying again until we get it right strengthens our emotional soul components and our overall character. With each succeeding cycle, we get stronger and smarter. We get wiser and more experienced; our emotional muscles metaphorically gain additional strength, tone, and endurance. We become stronger people through our failures, setbacks, and struggles if we learn from those challenges and make the necessary course adjustments along the way.

Recognize and write about your growth, and appreciate your progress. Share your experiences with others as you grow and succeed.

Upon studying and pondering these succinct and informative writings, Roger further considered his experiences with Edward Green, Bradley

Whitaker, and John Flagstaff, whom he had written about after reading the chapter *Mind-Set 4: Be Turned-Out and Win*. Despite their many serious life-changing setbacks, they learned to become *turned-out* by helping, teaching, and uplifting others. But the most impressive thing was that even to get to the point where they could become *turned-out*, they first needed to be converted to the idea of never giving in to self-pity and self-destruction. None of these three heroes ever gave up in their pursuit of happiness and success, despite debilitating diseases, crippling accidents, and sometimes being rejected and left to face their struggles on their own.

After reading and pondering these new thoughts and concepts from Billy Haynes about never giving up, Roger took a few more minutes for personal reflection. He recalled his ability to overcome the many frustrations and challenges in his preteen years while in grade school and junior high. Despite his physical, mental, and social limitations, he was determined to do well in sports and schoolwork, to make new friends, and to be a good friend. His own determination to improve and not give up in these areas was really important, but he also felt blessed and fortunate to have had a few influential people come into his life at critical times.

These saviors in their own right included an eighth grade history teacher, Mr. Beacom, who seemed to like Roger, and Ms. Trost, a high school history and writing teacher who took interest in his abilities and gave him strong encouragement to go on to college and excel there. Those acts of extra effort on their part and their level of interest was quite a change from the antipathy that Roger had felt from most of the other schoolteachers and principals prior to that time.

With Mr. Beacom, Roger felt that for the first time there was a teacher who actually liked him and was interested in his well-being. Mr. Beacom also made learning about US history interesting and exciting for Roger, for perhaps the first time. Roger was also fortunate to have Ms. Trost, as she gave him the extra time he needed to gain confidence in his abilities despite his many past academic discouragements.

Then there was Mrs. Jane Forester, a Sunday school teacher and the wife of Youth Pastor Gary Forester, who helped Roger gain an understanding of the spiritual side of his life. Through Forester's testimony of the Lord Jesus Christ, Roger gained the encouragement to pray and set spiritual goals, helping him to know that there was a God in the heavens who wanted him to succeed.

There were also football coaches, including Coach Houston and Coach Hoffer, who saw Roger's potential and found the right position for him to play, which was on defense instead of offense. Roger learned to be obedient to the tutelage of positive-minded teachers and coaches at the right time in his life and not to give up when it would have been easy to throw in the towel.

With those thoughts, Roger began to be aware of the time and his need to get back on track with the work at hand—work that would be challenging and difficult considering the weather and the setbacks he'd experienced the night before.

But with that *never give up* attitude that he had just been reminded of, Roger suddenly gained a renewed sense of optimism and a strong determination to find the scintillation counter and complete the radiological field monitoring. With that rekindled enthusiasm, he left the Tyler cabin at about 0815. He was fully prepared for cold and wet weather, being dressed in his thermal insulated rain gear and waterproof boots. He had also prepared his field pack with all the necessary equipment to resume his planned field monitoring activities, knowing that his confidence and positive mental attitude would give him the edge that day. The ground was still wet, and the morning air was a crispy thirty-eight degrees Fahrenheit. The golden sun was shining bright against the azure sky. The thick gray clouds had parted overnight, leaving a spectacular morning glow in a new setting.

After he found the trail that led to and from the Tyler cabin, Roger took a left turn, knowing that someplace within a good mile past the last mile marker would be the best place to start looking for the scintillation counter. With a brief glance back at the Tyler cabin, Roger he the heliport pad in a clearing about fifty feet to the west. In two days, that would be the pickup location where Tyler and Selos would fly in with the *Thunder Chicken* to end this adventurous expedition and safely carry Roger back to civilization.

Roger also remembered that there was no ham radio at the Tyler cabin. Therefore, there was no way for him to communicate with his clients to confirm the pickup time on Tuesday. He would just have to trust the last words he'd heard from Dr. Selos just four days before: *We'll pick you up at the Tyler cabin around noon on Tuesday.*

The last time Roger had walked this trail, it was very wet and pitch-dark, and he was following the illuminated Magnificent Mind-Set Man to the Tyler cabin, mesmerized by its glow. As a result, Roger was not completely sure if he could find the point along the trail where he would need to exit to his left to start searching for his lost instrument.

With that thought, he heard the cry of his patron eagle, the call of the wild, come again. As he looked in the direction of the eagle's cry, Roger was able to see his noble feathered friend gracefully gliding and circling over the dark green Douglas firs about seventy feet to his left.

Immediately Roger knew this was a sign that he should follow, and the eagle would lead him to the location where he had lost the scintillation counter the night before. With full confidence, Roger followed the cry and the circling eagle to a familiar place. As he peered ahead a few feet, in front him a beam of sunlight revealed a small, familiar-looking black case located between a rock and a large tree. *By golly, it's the scintillation counter case!* he thought.

As Roger approached and retrieved the object, he was very pleased and relieved. Upon opening the case, he found the meter intact, dry, and in excellent working order.

Uphill to the right was the general location where Roger had met Chloe face-to-face for the second time, and downhill to the left a ways was the place where he must have fallen while trying to shoot. Roger approached the short cliff where he'd been miraculously rescued by Billy, whereupon he was able to catch a spectacular clear panoramic view of the back side of Bokan Mountain, with the deep blue waters of Precipice Lake snugly tucked up against the base of the nearly thousand-foot granite-walled cliffs. The beautiful white and gray cliffs were further adorned with sporadic dark green speckles of dwarf fir trees jutting out from the cliff walls and the vertical black water stains streaking down the cliff walls from scores of thin waterfalls, some dry and others flowing, from one side of the cliff to the other.

In the years to come, Roger would claim this view as his favorite of all time and of all places. Compared to any other place on earth, this would be one of those *it's wherever you want it to be* memories vividly imprinted onto the file server of his mind.

In his days of preparation before visiting the island, when he was with the young Dr. Brundy, Roger had thoroughly studied topographic and geologic maps of the area. In addition, he had seen some amateurish photos taken of this side of Bokan Mountain and was casually aware of the beauty and uniqueness of this area, but he was largely unprepared to witness with his own eyes this once-in-a-lifetime vista of vistas. And he couldn't have known then of the absolutely ineffable impact that it would have on his mind and soul in the years to come. It was indeed a religious experience, as every fiber of his body resonated to give him a feeling of bliss, peace, and comfort. Roger thought, *If this is not the place where God himself lives or frequents, it should be.*

On the far side of the lake, Roger recognized the distinct topographic features known as the Seven Pools of Enlightenment of Precipice Lake. These pools had been named by people of the First Nations. According to a particular legend Roger had studied as part of his research, the pools were part of an ancient summer refuge for physically and mentally impaired people of the First Nations. Roger hoped in his heart and believed with his soul that this sacred peaceful area would remain undeveloped and never be disturbed or mined for commercial gain.

The ponds were simply seven smaller lakes, or roughly circular pools, about twenty-five to thirty-five feet in diameter and five to fifteen feet deep, which were naturally dammed with granitic rocks, boulders, and vegetation from along the small river that drained the mother lake, led downward, and meandered westward until it emptied into the Pacific Ocean about a half mile to the west. Each of the pools was at a slightly different elevation from the previous one, in a step-like fashion. White and gray dome-shaped granitic rocks that surrounded Precipice Lake and the Seven Pools were adorned with dark green clusters of Douglas firs jutting above the alpine landscape as high as twenty-five to thirty-five feet. This was a beautiful contrast that added to Roger's wondrous experience that day. This was the area where Roger would finish the radiological readings tomorrow and conclude the expedition as a whole on Tuesday.

But for the rest of the day on Sunday, he would need to survey the approximately sixty-acre outcrop of granite rocks in the Tyler cabin area. Then tomorrow, he would need a full day of hiking and surveying down and around the areas occupied by the Seven Pools of Enlightenment and Precipice Lake.

The surveying around the Tyler cabin was simple and straightforward, producing very low radiological values, which was what the team had anticipated for the area. The terrain mapping and the surveying were easy tasks that day; however, the weather was starting to tell a different story.

By noon the clouds returned, the winds picked back up, and colder temperatures again prevailed. By 1430, the cold rains and winds worsened to the point that working conditions were unbearable, but fortunately by that time, Roger had completed his survey and was only a couple of miles away from the cabin. Despite the bad weather, he was able to find the trail to the Tyler cabin with relative ease. He got back to shelter before sunset. The darkness made conditions dangerous.

The Tyler cabin was replete with food and wood fuel to keep Roger fed and warm for weeks, if needed. So with those provisions and comfort, he was able to complete his field notes for the day and have a savory beef stroganoff dinner. Such were the simple pleasures and necessities the cabin provided him. Upon retiring to bed at 2300, Roger was confident that he would get the rest he needed to be ready for his final full day on Prince of Wales Island.

CHAPTER 13

MIND-SET: 7 GROW FROM BASE TO GRACE

Monday, October 2 (Expedition - Day 8):
The Red Key Card

Roger slept very soundly for about three and a half hours, but he was suddenly awakened around 0230 by the glowing figurine of the Magnificent Mind-Set Man at the foot of his bed. A red puzzle piece on its head was brightly illuminated, with a white number 7 engraved in the center of the piece. The Mind-Set Man was repeatedly whispering the following sentence: *Roger, come with me and experience the Seven Divine Characteristics and complete your journey by learning the wisdom of the Seven Pools of Enlightenment of Precipice Lake.*

Upon Roger's exiting the Tyler cabin, the Magnificent Mind-Set Man suddenly disappeared. The dark night was instantaneously transformed into a beautiful clear day with the sun shining brightly as if this experience actually occurred during the morning of the following day. But Roger had no idea what day it was, if his emerging experience was real, or if he was in a deep and mysterious dream.

The next thing he knew, he was miles away from the Tyler cabin, standing near sea level at the edge of the forest and by a small river that emptied into the Pacific Ocean. He was clothed in basic field clothes; no coat was required since it was a mild day with temperatures in the midsixties. Roger felt compelled to follow the river upstream to determine where it would lead him and what he would learn. He continued following the little river up the slope toward the headwaters. It seemed to him that he hiked for several hours, climbing through countless twists and turns, small cliffs, and short waterfalls, and over fallen logs, rugged rocks, and bulging boulders. At length, he came to a sizable pool of sparkling clear water where the river was dammed in a shady thicket of tall Douglas firs. At this time of day, temperatures had risen into the mid to upper seventies. Roger had a strong, curious, and compelling desire to take off his shoes, roll up his pant legs, and wade in the cool and pure waters of this beautiful pool.

Upon entering the crystal clear waters, Roger felt a certain cleansing. Not only were his feet soothed in the cool waters, but also his whole soul seemed to be invigorated and enlightened with intelligence and wisdom. These feelings were augmented with another appearance of the Magnificent Mind-Set Man, which telepathically communicated several images and messages to Roger's mind.

The words of this illuminated figurine were as follows: *Roger, behold the Pool of Virtue, the waters of which you have entered. May you learn wisdom from these waters and apply the principle of virtue to your life so that you will greatly benefit from this this divine characteristic. May you always be possessed with this divine characteristic of virtue so that you may rise above the base things of this world on a road toward a higher plane of grace from this moment forward.*

With this admonition, Roger thought a thousand thoughts and articulated countless examples and applications of virtue that he had learned either on his own or through the example of others who had influenced him throughout his life. At that moment, he learned a wealth of wisdom concerning virtue that he had never before known or considered.

After pondering the many principles and concepts he had learned in that moment, Roger felt he should dry off, don his shoes, and resume his journey upriver toward additional opportunities for wisdom from the other pools of enlightenment that he suspected lay ahead.

Over the next several hours, Roger discovered six additional pools. Upon wading through each of their waters, he was just as enlightened by each one as he had been by the Pool of Virtue. After Roger waded in each, the Magnificent Mind-Set Man pronounced the same admonition and blessing for personal application and fulfillment to Roger's soul.

The Magnificent Mind-Set Man identified each successive pool as follows: the second pool was the Pool of Knowledge; the third, the Pool of Temperance; the fourth, the Pool of Patience; the fifth, the Pool of Kindness; the sixth, the Pool of Godliness; and the seventh, the Pool of Charity.

After experiencing and learning from the Pool of Charity, Roger hiked several more feet upstream along the river and beheld the beautiful and unforgettable waters of Precipice Lake with the backdrop of the cliffs and waterfalls on the west side of Bokan Mountain. The waters of the lake were still, as if frozen in time, and perfectly reflected the cliffs of Bokan Mountain in a timeless image that would live in the back of Roger's mind throughout the rest of his life.

At that moment, Roger awoke from his sleep sharply at 0700 by another loud call of the wild from his patron eagle, which came from just outside the Tyler cabin. *So it was a dream!* Roger thought as he began to get himself ready for his last full day on the island.

Then Roger remembered that he still possessed the red key card, the seventh of seven keys that he knew would open the Liberty safe and provide him with one last metal figurine and an additional set of Billy's writings. Using the red card, Roger eagerly open the safe before breakfast. As expected, he discovered a new metallic symbol and new set of writings.

The new figurine was a silver right angle about one foot by one foot in size, similar to a x- and y-axis. Written along the horizontal, or x-axis, was the word *base*, and written along the vertical, or y-axis, was the word *grace*. Between the x- and y-axes were seven steps rising from right to left. A word was written on each step as follows from right to left: Virtue, Knowledge, Temperance, Patience, Kindness, Godliness, and Charity.

Roger began reading the new writings.

From a Base State to a State of Grace MSA: Acquire the Seven Divine Characteristics

The word *base* in the context of this chapter is in reference to the world in its unrefined, corrupt, fallen, and decadent state. People who are in a state of baseness are selfish, self-absorbed, powerhungry, dishonorable, ignoble, sordid, corrupt, vile, immoral, mischievous, and dishonorable. A base person is in the state of the natural man or woman, and the natural man or woman is an enemy to God. Baseness leads to perpetual failure, sorrow, neglect, dereliction of duty, disbelief, lack of faith, and non-progression throughout life.

The natural man or woman left unchanged is subject to many forms of bad habits, crassness, and even various forms of dependency and addiction. Such addictions may include addiction to tobacco, alcohol, and drugs. Also, one may sexually abuse oneself and others, often initiated through addiction to pornography. People may be prone to gambling, idleness, video gaming, shopping, or compulsive eating—all of which I call voluntary slavery to a substance or a base desire.

Most of us have the tendency to fall into some of these characteristics of baseness if we do not choose to change, overcome, and rise above the natural man or woman inside us. This is where grace comes in.

Roger, you need to choose to overcome the base state or the mind-set of baseness. Grace is the antidote to baseness. To receive grace, you must have faith (i.e., believe in God and in humanity as the spiritual offspring of God). Faith leads to positive and edifying habits and the characteristics of humility, hope, and love. These characteristics are followed by charity, which is Christ's pure love, a love you can possess if you desire.

Roger, when you develop and cultivate grace in your life, by nature you will exhibit kindness, mercy, and benevolence. With grace, you will begin to believe you can make a difference, and you will strive through your spiritually reborn nature (your new nature) to better yourself and those around you. You make the pathway bright for yourself and others through your good works.

Grace and base are ninety degrees from each other. Think of the base state as being on a plane parallel to the earth, never rising above the earth and never ascending to greater heights. When we perpetually find ourselves somewhere along that plane, it is like we have lost the ability to improve and rise above the natural man.

Now, on the other hand, think of grace as being on a trajectory perpendicular to the base, a transcending meridian that rises far above the earth to celestial heights. In essence, because you strive to actively work to do good and improve yourself and the conditions around you, you begin to find divine gifts and new abilities to improve your life based on grace.

Concerning the comparison between the Lord, who is in heaven, and you and me, who are here on this mortal plane, Isaiah of the Old Testament once put it this way, citing the Lord's own words: *For my thoughts are not your thoughts, neither are your ways my ways, saith the Lord. For as the heavens are higher than the earth, so are my ways higher than your ways, and my thoughts than your thoughts* (Isaiah 55:8–9).

In order to contrast the baseness of the natural state of the world and of humankind versus the wisdom and grace of God, consider the seven base attributes, according to the wise Solomon, of the natural man or woman that will prevent you from ever being able to rise above the base plane of this world (Proverbs 6:16–19). These base attributes are as follows:

1. Proud looks – pride and self-centeredness, being truly *turned-in*
2. Lying tongues – lying and deceiving to build up the self because one loves oneself

3. Hands that shed innocent blood, the result of hate, anger, malice, and greed
4. A heart that devises wicked imaginations as a result of idleness
5. Swift feet running to mischief, including idleness and lust
6. False witness – lying, and hiding one's own faults instead repenting and resolving to improve
7. Sowing seeds of discord among brethren, the result of envy and contempt for others, as opposed to learning to love and serve others as the Lord has admonished us to do

These negative traits will prevent you from rising above worldly baseness because they are antithetical to developing the whole soul of a human being.

Let your enemies (entropy, your rivals, your competitors, etc.) be astonished by your rise from a base state to a state of grace. Let them be astonished by the fortress of goodness and righteousness you have erected, which is built upon the foundation of faith. And then add to your faith the following characteristics:

1. The walls of virtue
2. The reinforcement of knowledge
3. The fences of temperance
4. The buttresses of patience
5. The readiness and pro-activeness of kindness
6. The spiritual maintenance of godliness
7. The posture, poise, and grace of charity, which is the love of Christ in its purity and perfection

According to the apostle Peter (2 Peter 1:2–11), these seven characteristics are the key principles that define the ways and the acts of God himself. God challenges us to personally apply each of these divine characteristics in a methodical, step-by-step way based on a foundation of faith in him. According to Peter, the diligent application and realization of these characteristics will allow you to realize and cherish the following blessings and privileges:

- You will become a partaker of the divine nature of God (verse 4).
- You will receive the blessing of all things that pertain to life and godliness and receive of God's virtue and knowledge (verse 3).
- You will gain the ability to escape worldly corruption and lust (verse 4).
- You will be given the ability to make your calling and election of ultimate joy and happiness sure (verse 10).

This chief apostle then concludes that if you work diligently to develop these characteristics through study and application, *You shall never fall* (2 Peter 1:10).

Also, you must keep having faith, be confident in the fact that you were born to win, and know that your very being is made up of an aggregate of the five endowments of the human soul, as follows:

- heart (the spiritual gifts of the soul)
- might (the emotional gifts of the soul)
- mind (the mental gifts of the soul)
- strength (the physical gifts of the soul)
- social ability (the interactive gifts and abilities of the soul)

With this knowledge, you are better prepared to develop your whole soul by learning about and acquiring the seven divine characteristics Peter identified.

Roger, this is a two-step process: You start with a foundation of faith, knowing that you are a divine creation and were thus born to win. Then, with this knowledge and confidence, you apply each of the seven divine characteristics with all of you heart (spirituality), might (emotionality), mind (intellectuality), and strength (physicality), and with focused and effective social skills.

Roger, you have taken the opportunity to learn and experience wisdom and knowledge from each of the Seven Pools of Enlightenment of Precipice Lake, wherein you have received unique and wondrous lessons about and key insights into the seven divine characteristics. If you work diligently in each of these areas, these newly acquired characteristics will bless you throughout the rest of your life. In addition, these blessings will further enhance your life if you choose to share this enlightenment with others, particularly your family, friends, and neighbors.

The following pages are left blank so that you can use them to write about and share what you have learned from metaphorically wading in each of the Seven Pools of Enlightenment.

Upon reading the new writings, Roger recorded at the end of the BHIII memoirs what he could in the short period of time during breakfast about his impressions of and insights into each of the divine characteristics.

He knew that this would only be a start and that there could be volumes written on each of these divine characteristics. His brief writings were as follows:

The Pool of Virtue

As I waded in the Pool of Virtue, my mind reflected upon the divine characteristic of virtue. I was reminded by every component of my soul that virtue means wholeness as well as wholesomeness. As I practice and acquire aspects of virtue in my life, my eye will be focused with singleness of purpose and dedicated to my commitments to God, spouse, and family.

By adding my own thoughts and impressions to Billy's writings, I herein pledge and promise to myself, my spouse, my family, my neighbors, and my business associates that I will study, learn, and better apply the principle and characteristics of virtue more fully in my life.

Simultaneously, I will always do my best to practice honesty, integrity, authenticity, and sincerity. I will also continue to live a life of chastity, because my wife and family deserve to benefit from a relationship that is built upon trust, wholesomeness, and sound moral principles. It is therefore required that, to the absolute best of my ability, I put away and suppress any base desires that may from time to time creep into my mind and heart, leading to selfishness, unbridled emotions, lust, malice, envy, contempt, strife, and anger.

In terms of real application, I will utilize the principles of Mind-Set Technologies to improve in this area of my life; I will conduct a Mind-Set Evaluation (MSE) with respect to the current aspects of virtue in my life. I understand that there are physical, spiritual, emotional, mental, and social aspects of and implications to virtue. Therefore, I need to honestly evaluate where I am currently with respect to virtue in light of each of these components. Then I will set goals for change and proactively strive to adopt appropriate Mind-Set Adjustments (MSAs) that promote virtue in my life.

Having the divine characteristic of virtue as a functioning part of my life will bless me with a more successful, meaningful, abundant, and dynamic life and a closer and deeper relationship with my spouse, children, grandchildren, friends, neighbors, and work associates.

The Pool of Knowledge

As I waded in the Pool of Knowledge, my mind reflected upon knowledge as a divine characteristic. The Pool of Knowledge enhanced my understanding, and I was profoundly convinced that this divine characteristic includes more than just learning the basic academics or learning about formulas and compounds, facts and figures, mathematics and theorems, and science and methodologies. It is, in many ways, the means to spiritual and intellectual preparation and enlightenment. Furthermore, knowledge, as a divine characteristic, is more than gaining a grasp of certain concepts and ideas; knowledge also requires application and learned wisdom, even acquisition of transforming practical aspects that profoundly affect the whole soul of a man or woman, not just the intellectual side.

By adding my own thoughts and impressions to Billy's writings, I herein pledge and promise to myself, my spouse, my family, my neighbors, and my business associates that I will study, learn, and better apply the principles and characteristics of knowledge in order to more fully prepare myself for the more important aspects of life.

As I acquire knowledge, my eye will be focused on the important things in life. Thus, my preparation will be based on defining basic priorities. It is also required that I put away frivolous and irrelevant things and not watch too much television or participate in video or virtual-reality games. And I must suppress base desires—which will lead to selfishness, unbridled emotions, lust, malice, envy, contempt, strife, and anger—to the absolute best of my ability so that pure knowledge can flow uninhibited to my inner man, or core of my soul.

In terms of real application, I will commit to use the principles of Mind-Set Technologies; I will conduct an MSE with respect to how I currently gain knowledge in my life. I understand that there are physical, spiritual, emotional, mental, and social aspects of and implications to knowledge. Therefore, I need to couple my knowledge MSE with honesty and evaluate where I am currently with these components. Then I will set goals for change and proactively strive for, work toward, and adopt appropriate MSAs to gain more appropriate knowledge that is aligned with my ultimate goals.

Having the divine characteristic of knowledge as a functioning part of me will bless me with a more focused and meaningful life and a closer and deeper relationship with my spouse, children, grandchildren, friends, neighbors, and work associates.

The Pool of Temperance

As I waded in the Pool of Temperance, I began to more fully appreciate the concept of temperance as a divine characteristic. I was reminded that sobriety, self-control, and self-mastery are qualities that allow for greater degrees of virtue and knowledge to prevail in my soul. Temperance, as a divine characteristic, will also help me be naturally *turned-out*. This is profoundly true, because a temperate person by definition is not enslaved by or bound to addictive behaviors and substances that otherwise keep a person *turned-in* and heading toward deadend avenues based on perpetual failure, selfishness, and greed.

By adding my own thoughts and impressions to Billy's writings, I herein pledge and promise to myself, my spouse, my family, my neighbors, and my business associates that I will study, learn, and apply the principles and characteristics of temperance more fully in my life.

If I am a temperate person, I will have more freedom, agency, and control over the situations of my life. I can and will remain a non-gambler, even though I will always be a gambling addict. I can also control my personal and emotional weather forecast with a positive mental attitude, and with sunshine in my soul, destructive storms will be held at bay.

As I practice temperance in my life by shunning all forms of addictive substances, including drugs, tobacco, and alcohol, and by avoiding other traps and vices, such as pornography, gambling, eating disorders, excessive shopping, spending inordinate amounts of time in front of the television, and video gaming, my soul can become filled with many good things, if I choose to pursue them. Also, my eye will be more focused and dedicated to my commitments to God, spouse, and family. I will be more likely to bless my life with unselfish endeavors by having more time and the mental, emotional, and spiritual desire to serve and bless the lives of others.

In terms of real application, I will commit to use the principles of Mind-Set Technologies; I will conduct an MSE with respect to living a temperate life, let moderation and balance in all things prevail in my life, and carefully evaluate my habits. Thus, I will find myself making positive and lasting changes to establish constructive rather than destructive behaviors.

I understand that there are physical, spiritual, emotional, mental, and social aspects of and implications to living a temperate life. Therefore, I need to evaluate my temperance MSE and honestly evaluate where I am currently in light of these components. Then I will set goals for change and proactively strive for, work toward, and adopt appropriate MSAs with respect to temperance.

The Pool of Patience

As I waded through the Pool of Patience, I was reminded that patience is something that is not natural in the world. In particular, patience as a divine characteristic is extremely rare.

As I strive to practice and acquire aspects of patience in my life, my eye will be focused, of single purpose, and dedicated to my commitments to God, spouse, and family. I will always practice being patient with myself and others in a sincere and authentic manner.

By adding my own thoughts and impressions to Billy's writings, I hereby pledge and promise to myself and my spouse, my family, my neighbors, and my business associates that I will study, learn, and apply the principles and characteristics of patience more fully in my life. If I am patient with others, I will find that others will naturally be patient with me.

In terms of real application, I will use the principles of Mind-Set Technologies; I will conduct an MSE with respect to patience. I understand that there are physical, spiritual, emotional, mental, and social aspects of and implications to patience. Therefore, in my MSE I need to honestly evaluate where I am currently in these components. Then I will set goals for change and proactively strive for, work toward, and adopt appropriate MSAs with respect to patience.

Having the divine characteristic of patience as a functioning part of me will bless me with a happier and more meaningful life and allow me to become closer to my spouse, children, grandchildren, friends, neighbors, and work associates.

The Pool of Kindness

As I waded through the Pool of Kindness, I was reminded that the divine characteristic of kindness, like the characteristic of patience, is not a natural thing of this world, but is a rare and precious characteristic.

I was reminded with every component of my soul that kindness means goodness and pureness to self and others. As I practice and acquire aspects of kindness in my life, my eye will be focused, of single purpose, and dedicated to my commitments to God, spouse, and family.

I will always practice being kind to others, including my family, my relatives, my neighbors, my workmates, and even strangers. I should also be kind to myself and practice not being so hard on myself for my actual and perceived peccadillos. I should also not judge others for their offenses and eccentricities. I need to remember the power of one of the Lord's beatitudes: *Blessed are the merciful: for they shall obtain mercy* (Matthew 5:7). This means that if I avoid being harsh with others, somehow, maybe, others will not be so harsh with me. Even the Lord will be more merciful to me on Judgment Day because of the mercy I show to others.

In terms of real application, I will use the principles of Mind-Set Technologies; I will conduct an MSE with respect to the aspects of kindness in my life currently. I understand that there are physical, spiritual, emotional, mental, and social aspects of and implications to kindness. Therefore, in my kindness MSE I will need to honestly evaluate where I am currently in light of these components. Then I will set goals for change and proactively strive for, work toward, and adopt appropriate MSAs with respect to kindness.

By adding my own thoughts and impressions to Billy's writings, I herein pledge and promise to myself and my spouse, family, neighbors, and business associates that I will study, learn, and apply the principles and characteristics of kindness more fully in my life.

Having the divine characteristic of kindness as a functioning part of me will bless me with a and more meaningful life and a closer and deeper relationship with my spouse, children, grandchildren, friends, neighbors, and work associates.

The Pool of Godliness

As I waded through the Pool of Godliness, I was reminded of the divine characteristic of godliness.

As I practice and acquire aspects of godliness in my life, my eye will be focused, of single purpose, and dedicated to my commitments to God, spouse, and family. I will always strive to practice godliness and acquire godly characteristics and do so with, honesty, integrity, authenticity, and sincerity. It is also required that, to the absolute best of my ability, I put away and suppress base desires, which lead to selfishness, unbridled emotions, lust, malice, envy, contempt, strife, and anger.

George Washington did not become a successful leader by just showing up one day. He had years of preparation in farming, surveying, and martial and political leadership. One of the greatest things that General Washington was able to do in his life was to practice and acquire habits and behaviors of etiquette, personal hygiene, and politeness. There was a refining process that took years and led him to develop positive and even godlike behaviors that built him up as a model of personal and social success.

In terms of real application, I will use the principles of Mind-Set Technologies; I will conduct an MSE with respect to the aspects of godliness in my life currently. I understand that there are physical, spiritual, emotional, mental, and social aspects of and implications to the practice of godliness. Therefore, in my MSE, I will need to honestly evaluate where I am currently in light of these components. Then I will set goals for change and proactively strive for, work toward, and adopt appropriate MSAs with respect to godliness.

By adding my own thoughts and impressions to Billy's writings, I herein pledge and promise to myself and my spouse, family, neighbors, and business associates that I will study, learn, and apply the principles and characteristics of godliness more fully in my life.

Having the divine characteristic of godliness as a functioning part of me will bless me with a more meaningful life and a closer and deeper relationship with my spouse, children, grandchildren, friends, neighbors, and work associates.

The Pool of Charity

As I waded through the Pool of Charity, I was blessed with a greater understanding of charity than I had ever considered before.

With respect to the divine characteristic of charity, I was reminded with every component of my soul that charity is something you have that enables and motivates you to give. Having charity is not necessarily giving things to the needy; it is having love, which motivates you to do good to others.

If you possess charity, then you possess love, even perfect and pure love, which motivates you to do good to others. These good acts include, but are not limited to, giving of your substance to those who lack and stand in need. You give because of the love that you have perfected. Christ loved and gave, thereby showing you how to love and give. So, you love and give as he did.

As I practice and acquire aspects of charity in my life, my eye will be focused, of single purpose, and dedicated to my commitments to God, spouse, family, and neighbors. I will practice loving and giving with honesty, integrity, authenticity, and sincerity.

By adding my own thoughts and impressions to Billy's writings, I herein pledge and promise myself and my spouse, family, neighbors, and business associates that I will study, learn, and apply the principles and characteristics of charity more fully in my life.

In terms of real application, I will use the principles of Mind-Set Technologies; I will conduct an MSE with respect to the aspects of charity in my life currently. I understand that there are physical, spiritual, emotional, mental, and social aspects and implications to charity. Therefore, in my charity MSE, I will honestly evaluate where I am at currently in these components. Then I will set goals for change and proactively strive, work, and adopt appropriate MSAs with respect to charity.

Having the divine characteristic of charity as a functioning part of me will bless me with a more meaningful life and a closer and deeper relationship with my spouse, children, grandchildren, friends, neighbors, and work associates.

CHAPTER 14

THE RESCUE ON BOKAN MOUNTAIN

Roger became aware of the time, which was becoming more and more of a critical factor as the morning wore on. He promised himself that he would set a goal to spend significantly more time considering each of the seven divine characteristics and write about each in more detail at a later date. He needed to get back to the tasks at hand, which were to collect more radiological data near Precipice Lake and its associated Seven Pools of Enlightenment. His work for the day also included one additional mining cave, along the west side of the lake and adjacent to the cliffs on the northwest side of Bokan Mountain. A little voice in his mind reminded him again that he needed to get rolling because he had a lot of ground to cover and just one day to finish up the monitoring before returning to the Tyler cabin. There he would spend the night, and in the morning he would prepare to be picked up sometime around noon by Tyler and Selos in the *Thunder Chicken*.

To Roger's knowledge, the Tyler-area mining cave, which was known as the Tyler Cave, was never actively or successfully mined for any appreciable amounts of uranium ore or any metals or natural resources that would be considered profitable. Instead, it was more of an extensive exploration cave for the Tyler-Haynes uranium team at the climax of uranium mining activities in the late 1980s. Nevertheless, this feature was part of Roger's scope of work, just to make sure the new mining team knew where the mine waste rock did and did not exist in each of the claimed areas around Bokan Mountain. If nothing else, it was just for the record.

So in accordance with the plan, Roger thoroughly packed up his equipment and left the Tyler cabin by 0845 that Monday morning, October 2. He needed to take the well-marked trail that led about four and a half to five miles down from the Tyler cabin to the mouth of Precipice River, where the river, which was the main drainage from Precipice Lake, emptied into the Pacific Ocean.

He then needed to follow a more difficult and even treacherous trail up and alongside Precipice River, through each of the Seven Pools of Enlightenment below Precipice Lake and collect radiological measurements every 100 to 200 feet. This required that he hike through rugged terrain—around trees, over tree roots, through sometimes thick vegetation, and over large, slippery moss-covered granite boulders—as he climbed about 875 vertical feet for about one and a half miles. In addition, he would be carrying his pack, which weighed somewhere between twenty-five and thirty pounds, loaded with equipment, supplies, food, and water.

Then he needed to hike around the west side of Precipice Lake for about two more miles to the Tyler Cave, through rocky, though relatively even, terrain, and continue collecting and recording radiological data every one hundred to two hundred feet until he got to the Tyler Cave entrance. Then he was required to collect radiological data inside the cave every ten feet for about one hundred feet, which was the anticipated length of the cave.

The hike down the trail to the mouth of the river was well marked and all downhill. The trip down went quickly and was without incident. Temperatures remained in the low to mid-forties, and a light rain was falling, a little here and there along the way, so weather was not as much of a factor as it had been the last couple of days.

It took Roger only a little over two hours to hike the trail to the end of the river where it emptied into the ocean, and another two and a half hours to climb up the river's side, taking radiological measurements at the appropriate intervals and passing each of the Seven Pools of Enlightenment, for a total of four and a half hours to reach Precipice Lake.

A very comforting and ethereal feeling came over Roger as he approached the first pool, which he recognized as the Pool of Virtue. Strangely, every detail seemed to be the same in person as it had been in his dream the night before, even though he had never physically been to this location before. The resemblance included everything from the trees and rocks down to the very size and shape of the pool itself.

Upon reaching the edge of the Pool of Virtue, Roger again heard the cry of his patron eagle and then immediately spotted his companion flying around the top of the tallest Douglas fir along the side of the pool. This familiar experience gave him the intellectual, emotional, and spiritual ability to recall precisely all the thoughts, feelings, and insights he had experienced the night before during his dream when he metaphorically waded in this same pool—only under warmer conditions.

In haste, and with energy and enthusiasm, Roger hiked up the hill and through the rugged terrain of large granitic rocks, thick brush, and fallen trees throughout the rest of the morning and into the afternoon, progressing sequentially to the second, third, fourth, fifth, sixth, and seventh pools. As he approached each pool, he immediately recognized each one, down to the last detail.

He recognized the second pool as the Pool of Knowledge, the third pool as the Pool of Temperance, the fourth pool as the Pool of Patience, the fifth pool as the Pool of Kindness, the sixth pool as the Pool of Godliness, and the seventh pool as the Pool of Charity. Upon approaching each pool, he felt a familiar feeling of calm and ethereal peace. The gifts of peace, comfort, and remembrance that he'd experienced because of his patron eagle lingered with him throughout that day at the edge of each of the Seven Pools of Enlightenment.

Just being present at the edge of each pool, along with the comforting cry of his patron eagle, gave Roger the ability to continue to build upon his profound understanding of the divine characteristics of virtue, knowledge, temperance, patience, kindness, godliness, and charity.

Countless examples of how he could improve his life in each of these areas came storming into Roger's mind. In an instant, he was able to reason and understand how he could work more diligently and strive to excel in each of these areas with respect to the five whole-soul components of his life: physical, spiritual, mental, emotional, and social. His desire was to acquire and improve upon each of these characteristics to greatly improve his personal life and enhance his relationships with his family, friends, neighbors, and business acquaintances.

On the spot, Roger began formulating and outlining several goals in his mind, and he planned how he could achieve these goals in the most appropriate and reasonable time frame. He vowed that as soon as he could, he would write down each specific goal in his journal and create reasonable time lines to begin achieving success with respect the seven divine characteristics.

At the conclusion of these miraculous and unforgettable experiences, which took place over the span of only a few minutes at each pool, Roger spent about fifteen to twenty minutes collecting radiological data from the rocks. The field activities were conducted in accordance with his plan for the day. Based on the readings, he noted that there was abnormally high radiological activity in these areas, growing stronger with each succeeding pool, from the base near sea level all the way up to Precipice Lake. From Roger's interpretation of the data, these anomalous readings indicated that the rocks deep beneath each pool could be conducive to future exploration; there could be profitable radioactive ore in these areas. He was sure that Tyler and Selos would be thrilled with this data, knowing that this area could potentially pay future dividends should they have the desire ever to begin mining here. But Roger hoped that development would never occur in this sacred place.

Roger also noted, as he continued taking the readings around the lake and at Tyler Cave, that radiological activity began to decrease sharply, becoming almost nil by the time he reached the cave. The readings were nearly zero inside Tyler Cave, which was a very dark, cold, and dank place. It was also a very narrow cave—only about seven to ten feet wide. The pathway inward, including several twists and turns, went for about one hundred feet in length, all the way to the back of the cave.

Roger could not wait to get out of the Tyler Cave, finish up his work for the entire investigation, and get back to the warm Tyler cabin. More than anything else, he wanted to get a good night's rest during his last night on Prince of Wales Island. But when he was only halfway out of the cave, the ground suddenly shook, probably from a moderate earthquake or a landslide down the steep banks of Bokan Mountain.

Whatever it was, it jolted Roger with enough force to knock him completely off his feet and onto the cave floor. Several rocks dislodged from the ceiling of the cave and hit Roger on the head. And then several rocks fell onto his legs—bruising, cutting, and crushing him, pinning him to the floor of the cave.

The shaking lasted only about thirty-five to forty seconds, but it was enough to start the rockfall injuring Roger and putting his life in jeopardy. The temperature in the Tyler Cave was only about fifty degrees, but with Roger being temporarily knocked out for about twenty minutes, he was subject to hypothermia and potential shock on account of his injuries. His flashlight was damaged, inoperable, and nowhere to be found once he partially awoke from his brief coma.

So there he was, at the end of his expedition, stunned and in pain in a wet, cold, and dark cave, not exactly lucid or even fully aware of the danger he was in. Over the span of the next thirty to forty minutes, Roger just lay still in a daze. A growing feeling of discomfort and then despair began to seize him. He began praying to God for protection and deliverance, but his faith slowly began to fail him. He just wanted to get back safely to Salt Lake City and be in the loving arms of his beautiful wife Julie.

Then moments later, in answer to his prayers, Roger noticed a dim yellow light coming toward him, which he could barely see at first but which gradually seemed to be getting brighter and brighter. Finally Roger could faintly make out the blurry figure of an old man with a pack on his back, holding a lantern in one hand and a steaming pot in the other, standing within five feet of him.

Then Roger heard a voice, which he thought he recognized, say in a gravelly whisper, *Well, Roger, you really got yourself in a fix this time, didn't you?*

Who is it? Who are you? Roger was still half dazed at this point. *It's Billy Haynes again, Roger. Who else do you think it is? I'm here with a warm blanket, water, a hot pot of beef stew, and good company from an old trusty friend.*

Roger, being confused, disoriented, and in pain, was still trying to figure out what had happened. *What's going on? What was that jolt that caused the cave-in?*

That shaking you felt was a 7.1 earthquake over a hundred miles north of here in a remote part of mainland Alaska. It was just enough to produce the jolt you felt and the cave-in.

Billy then slowly unpinned Roger from beneath a small pile of several midsized rocks, causing Roger to shout out in pain, but also giving him a feeling of relief and freedom from the burden and confinement. Billy then promptly reached into Roger's pack, which he had pulled off his back, and took out a first aid kit. Bringing out a pair of scissors first, Billy gently cut off Roger's left pant leg from the thigh down, exposing the injured leg but leaving his sock and boot on. Then Billy applied a balm of antibacterial ointment, which he followed with a series of clean gauze bandages to dress Roger's lacerations and bruises.

There you go, Roger! You should be feeling better soon. Here, take these two Tylenol tablets with this water from my canteen. That should help with the pain, Billy said, slowly propped up Roger so he could take the pills.

Billy wrapped Roger in one quilt and then pulled out two more. One he folded up into a crude but somewhat effective pillow that he placed under Roger's head, and the other he ever so carefully placed under Roger's quivering body. *This quilted blanket should keep you warm for the rest of the night. I will stay with you tonight until you fall sleep, and then I will flag down the helicopter in the morning. You'll be all right, Roger, I promise you. Just lie back and try to relax.*

Roger was further comforted once he noticed that the quilt placed over him was his favorite LA Dodgers blanket from the Tyler cabin;

it quickly provided his body with the warmth that he so desperately needed.

Billy continued to keep Roger engaged in light conversation about the work that he had completed and then began to spoon-feed Roger the hot stew from the pot he'd carried in with him.

As Roger began to feel comforted, and as the pain began to ease, he collected himself enough to formulate some questions for Billy. *How do you know?*

How do I know what? asked Billy.

How do you know when I am in trouble and need help? You seem to know when I need help and what help I need. Almost immediately. You're always close by, but I never know you're there until I need the help. And then all the metallic key cards, the safe, the figurines, and your writings. You have written these things to me and for me even though we don't even know each other and have never met. Are you even a real live person, or are you a ghost—or a guardian angel? How are you able to do these things and why? Why me, Billy?

A moment went by without an immediate reply or answer. Then Billy began with several comforting words. *Well, Roger, I can't give you the answers to all of your questions, because it would probably blow your mind, and you would never believe it all anyway. But what I can say is that I have been teaching you and protecting you because I am allowed to, and because I need you to learn from your failures and mistakes, overcome your self-pity, put away your many bad habits, and forever bury your gambling addiction. I need you to remember the things you learned from the Magnificent Mind-Set Man and from my writings during the last week and a half here on the slopes of Bokan Mountain. I need you to write about them, apply them, and teach them to others. The world needs to hear these things, Roger.*

Okay, but why did you choose me, Billy? You don't know anything about me.

Oh? But I do know you, Roger! Billy answered.

I don't remember ever meeting you! Roger replied.

You're wrong, Roger. We have met before. I know a lot more about you than you think.

When? Where have we met? Roger asked.

Roger, think back to about twenty- two years ago, when you were on your way to Egypt as a graduate student. On that all-night flight in a TWA Boeing 747 from New York to Cairo, don't you remember sitting next to an older man who asked you about your goals, aspirations, and philosophy of life? We talked about spiritual things, like the purpose of life, and academic things, like business ethics and geology. You told me about your upcoming studies in Egypt and said that you had been selected by the university to conduct two months of fieldwork for your master's thesis. The work would be in the Fayum region, on the paleoecology and depositional environments of the rocks in that area. Billy paused for a moment and then continued. *That was me, Roger.*

Roger did not answer immediately. He just looked to be in a deep stupor of thought.

After a moment of silence, Billy continued with further reminiscence.

Roger, I was deeply impressed with your enthusiasm, your faith in God, and your strong desire to succeed. I was so inspired by your positive outlook on life and your ambitious goals that I thought of offering you a job after your graduation to work with me as an entry-level geologist for my mining consulting firm. I tried to give you my business card at the Cairo airport after landing, but we got separated in the crowd and I never saw you again, until of course I spotted you on the island and noticed your name on some of the paperwork in my cabin.

You see, I watch and monitor everyone who comes and stays here at Prince of Wales Island, looking for someone I can trust, teach, and inspire in ways that cannot be explained by natural laws or normal conditions. It may be hard for you to understand, and it may not make sense, Roger, but I have been endowed with heavenly powers to communicate and share my concepts of success and Mind-Set Technologies with anyone of my choice.

Roger continued to lie in his injured position and listen with intent interest as Billy continued providing additional explanations.

I tried with some of the others who have worked here from time to time, but none of your predecessors had been in tune enough with spiritual things to ever catch on to what I was trying to teach them. With each of them, I would always find that continuing was a futile effort because of their lack of faith and humility. Then, when I saw you here and remembered our deep discussions over thirty years ago, I decided to choose you.

I chose you to receive my writings because I can see what's in your heart. I decided to test you, protect you, and give you the opportunity to learn about and benefit from the concepts of the Mind-Set Technologies and the Seven Transcending Mind-Sets of Success. You seem to have a sense about and an appreciation for spiritual things, and enough humility to be taught and to learn wisdom to a greater degree than most of the others I have been trying to influence for over fifteen years on this beautiful sacred mountain.

As Roger became more and more convinced that he and Billy had met years ago, he began asking additional questions about his role in moving his life forward.

So, what do you want me to do Billy?

I want you to apply these concepts, expand upon them, and then write about them. Maybe you can even write a book about these things and teach others these ideas, so that many others can prosper as I have from these wonderful concepts.

With remaining self-doubt, Roger begged for more answers. *So how do I know where to go from here?*

Roger, if you ponder and apply the teachings you have learned over the last ten days, your life will change for the better. You will find a greater strength within you to deal with your stress, struggles, insecurities, and gambling addiction in positive ways. You will be greatly blessed as you teach others the concepts, analogies, and lessons you have experienced on this mountain. As a recovering gambling addict, you can help others in their recovery process and give personal examples of overcoming challenges and adopting new mind-sets.

Hold on a second, Billy. How do you know about my struggles and addiction?

The fact that I know this about you, Roger, should convince you that you are being given a divine opportunity and blessing to help yourself and others.

Go home, Roger. Share all of your experiences with your wife. Write about these things and formulate a plan to share them with others. You need to realize that as you do these things with enthusiasm, you will become a

Magnificent Mind-Set Man in your own right. You will be blessed with more success than you could ever imagine!

So you have two choices, Roger. Choose to apply and share these experiences, or don't. This is your fork-in-the-road moment. You can either choose to live a better life with these concepts applied and taught, or you can choose to do nothing and continue to live an unhappy and mediocre life. You know, Roger, you have been tempted a lot lately to return to gambling. All the signs are there, and you are going to need to apply these new mind-sets to keep you on the wagon.

Billy continued his monologue with a few admonitions.

If you do nothing, then nothing good will happen in your life! So the last question I have for you, Roger, is ...Billy paused a few short seconds, closed one eye, cocked his head slightly, puckered his lips, and asked, Whatcha gonna do about it?

As Roger pondered in silence for a moment to capture Billy's promises and admonitions, everything suddenly came to him in an instant.

Wait a minute! That was you on the plane, wasn't it?

Billy didn't answer, but Roger continued.

That was indeed you, you strange old man! I remember now! And I also remember seeing you carrying a strange alabaster box as we parted ways at the Cairo International Airport, just like the one ... Roger paused as he recalled. Just like the box I found and lost twice! The box that held the key cards!

At that moment, Billy silently began to collect his pack and other things. Then he mysteriously disappeared, leaving behind the lantern, food, water, and other necessities to keep Roger comfortable for the night.

Given his fatigue and the fact that it had been a long day for him, Roger fell helplessly asleep for the night. He slept until he was suddenly awakened by Tyler and Selos at about 1045 the next morning.

These two rescuers suddenly appeared in front of Roger, tapping him on his shoulder and begging him to awake. They carried him out of the Tyler Cave and into the idling *Thunder Chicken*, which had landed in a flat clearing about a hundred feet from the cave.

Once the men were safely aboard the *Thunder Chicken*, Keiffer Selos put the mic and earphone headset on Roger's head. As they flew off, Keiffer helped him with his gear, monitoring equipment, and then his seat belt. Suddenly, as Roger opened his eyes, he noticed that all four seats were filled onboard, with the fourth seat being occupied by his colleague Kurt Brundy, who gave him a warm smile and a nod of the head, indicating a sincere, warm, and affectionate greeting, as well as a nonverbal proclamation of a job well done.

Brundy of course had undergone quite an ordeal of his own by enduring an emergency appendectomy and having a near-death experience only about a week previously. *Apparently he has recovered sufficiently to take the ride out to the island,* Roger thought.

Not long into the flight, Selos began pestering Roger with questions: *Who was the old man who shot off the flare guns and flagged us down near your location? When we arrived at the Tyler cabin this morning, we noticed that you were not there, and none of your equipment was either, so we started flying around the Precipice Lake area to find you, thinking you had finished up your work a short distance away from the planned point of rendezvous. We then spotted several flares shot into the air in this area. We saw an old man frantically waving red flags above his head, signaling us to land as close and as soon as possible. By the time we found a safe spot to land the Thunder Chicken and had set it down over there, we couldn't find the old-timer, but we soon found the flags posted in the ground just in front of the Tyler Cave. That is when we entered the cave and found you. Your leg was perfectly bandaged up. It looks like someone was taking good care of you. Who was that old man, Roger?*

It was Billy Haynes! replied Roger. *It was none other than Billy himself*!

No one said a word in reply, their mouths gaping wide open.

CHAPTER 15

THE FINAL AWAKENING

With a piercing scream of a bald eagle, Roger Hunt was suddenly awakened and found himself in the Black Pearl, parked on the shoulder of State Highway 51 in southern Idaho. With this call of the wild, Roger came to himself and realized that he was back to the current time in early February 2016—and that in one night he had mysteriously relived an experience that he'd had nearly ten years ago. He knew in his heart that it was an experience that he should have benefited from but had not. The call of the wild that awakened Roger caused him to remember all the important details he had dreamed about during the night. Every detail of each those experiences was embedded into his mind and heart in an instant of time, as if he had actually relived every moment in every detail.

He vividly remembered all about the figurines and symbols and the BHIII memoirs. The Magnificent Mind-Set Man figurine, which had mysteriously guided Roger and taught him the important concepts of the Seven Transcending Mind-Sets of Success, appeared in his mind's eye. Each of the puzzle pieces illuminated in sequence: MST, MSE, MSA. Roger immediately remembered each of the corresponding concepts of Mind-Set Technologies by conducting Mind-Set Evaluations, followed by learning how to make important Mind-Set Adjustments. Then, as this vision continued, the Magnificent Mind-Set Man figurine began illuminating in sequence each of the seven acronyms: BTW, DEW, F.A.I.R., TI-TO, BPS, NGU, and BTG. As Roger focused on each of these, he immediately recalled the meaning and application of each.

When he focused on the BTW piece, Roger also remembered the white porcelain figurine of two caring hands gently holding an infant, which represented the Born to Win MSA. He recalled all the details and applications of this important mind-set. He felt joy and confidence because he knew in his mind and heart that he had been born with divine endowments and gifts to give him the confidence that he needed to overcome his trials and succeed.

When he focused on the DEW piece, Roger immediately remembered the metallic figurine of the red apple with a bite taken out of each side and with a slash running through the letter *E*, which he knew stood for the Defeat Entropy and Win MSA. Then he recalled that if he used each of the whole-soul components (physical, spiritual, intellectual, emotional, and social) of his life, he could learn to proactively overcome the negative effects of entropy (or natural tendencies toward disorder) in his life and succeed.

When he focused on the F.A.I.R. piece, Roger immediately remembered the metallic figurine of a round magnifying glass with F.A.I.R. embedded within the lens and knew that it stood for the F.A.I.R. principles of setting goals to achieve success. He recalled that he should effectively set both ultimate and supporting goals by focusing on the most appropriate and pertinent goals that would make a difference in his life. He also remembered the importance of having a winning attitude or positive mental attitude (PMA) in order to achieve his goals; investing his time, talents, and financial means into his goals; and aligning himself with things that are relevant, versus irrelevant, to his goals.

When he focused on the TI-TO piece, Roger remembered the flat metallic dislike object with a small circular center and sixteen curved arrows, eight emanating outward and eight pointing inward. He immediately recalled the significance of being *turned-out* versus *turned-in* and serving others and overcoming selfish desires to gain a more positive perspective on life. He remembered his true-life experiences with John Flagstaff, Bradly Whitaker, and Ed Green, each of whom experienced tragedies beyond imagination but chose to remain *turned-out* and serve others despite their great trials and setbacks. Roger knew that if these gentlemen could be *turned-out*, then he could as well, no matter his circumstances.

When he focused on the PBS piece, Roger remembered the metallic figurine of a man's hand firmly grasping a single bolt of lightning. He immediately recalled that this symbol stood for controlling one's personal emotional weather forecast. It reminded him that he had the power to call for peace in order to calm the personal emotional storms that sometimes beset him.

When he focused on the NGU piece, Roger remembered the hand-sized model of two ski poles, a soccer ball, and a baseball bat welded together in one continuous piece, with a karate black belt holding the three pieces together. He recalled that this symbol stood for Never Give Up, no matter one's circumstances. It also represented his children in their youth, all of whom never gave up and kept trying and competing in their choice of team and individual sports and also endured their individual trials to become responsible adults who contributed to society. Roger rejoiced in their achievements and respected their courage.

When he focused on the BTG piece, Roger remembered the Base to Grace metallic figurine in the shape of a right angle with seven steps representing the seven divine characteristics taught by the apostle Peter in the New Testament. He also remembered the Seven Pools of Enlightenment, each of which stood for one of the seven divine characteristics: virtue, knowledge, temperance, patience, kindness, godliness, and charity. When he pondered how he could set goals and improve in each of these areas, he felt great love and support from on high.

After experiencing this marvelous recapitulation of all that he had learned previously, Roger felt encouraged, invigorated, and eager to get to Boise that morning. He wanted to find a hotel where he could check in early and begin writing about all the things he'd just relived, before catching a flight to Anchorage later that evening. He also wanted to call Julie and begin sharing with her the marvelous secrets he had kept from her all these years because of pride and self-doubt that he could make transforming changes and impose those concepts on others.

He knew he had been given a second chance to improve himself and his relationship with his wife and his adult children in ways that would totally transcend all his previous efforts. He also knew that these new mind-sets would give him a better chance to never again succumb to his gambling addiction. They would be a springboard, helping him to help himself and giving him the tools and insights to help others with similar struggles.

The next thing Roger knew, his cell phone was ringing. Upon answering, he realized from the number that appeared on his screen that it was Kurt Brundy calling, the same young professor from Anchorage, Alaska, whom he had not seen or heard from in ten years.

Roger, is that you? Did I get the right number?

Yes, it's me. This is Roger Hunt. Kurt! How the heck are you, my old friend? Roger was in a state of amazement and joy to hear Kurt's voice again and upon learning he was evidently doing well.

Roger, listen to me closely. We need to meet again sometime, sometime real soon! I need to tell you about an experience that I just had, and I need you to help me understand some things. I think you are the only one who can answer my questions!

What can I help you with, Kurt?

As part of the University of Alaska Anchorage, I was recently retained by Selos and Tyler, if you can believe those two old fossils are still alive and working. They hired me to collect updated radiological data on Bokan Mountain. To make a long story short, I have spent the last week out there, as you did ten years ago. While out there, I experienced some fascinating things—incredible things, to say the least.

Oh? What kind of things?

Roger, try to recall back ten years ago as I bring you up to date on my life. Metallic key cards, mysterious figurines, a figurine of a man's head—which for some reason I'm compelled to call the Magnificent Mind-Set Man—and sudden Billy Haynes sightings. Do any of these things sound familiar to you or ring a bell in any way?

Are you kidding me, Kurt? You too?

Roger, I am a little pressed for time right now, so when do you think we can get together and discuss these things? Kurt continued before Roger could answer. You know what I am talking about, don't you, Roger?

Yes, as a matter of fact, I do, Roger replied.

Kurt continued, *You know, Roger, Billy spoke to me on Bokan Mountain and said that you and I need to reconnect and team up to get this message out to the world. I agree with him, Roger! You know you can't keep quiet about these things any longer, right? Especially since I know them now as well. We have to get together, share notes, and start writing and teaching these things to people. We need to reach out to business leaders who want to improve their companies, parents who are struggling with their children, people who just need more direction in life, people with depression, and thousands of others who are having problems with dependency and addiction. The world is waiting for these magnificent things, Roger!*

Roger eagerly responded, *Kurt, I know you are right, and as a matter of fact, I am traveling up to Anchorage on an Alaska Airlines flight later tonight from Boise. Are you available for lunch tomorrow?*

Kurt answered with courage and enthusiasm. *I am, Roger— let's do it!*

ABOUT THE BOOK

The Magnificent M ind -Set Man will inspire you to be the person you want to be, the person you know you should be, the person you know you could be and will be—if you choose to be.

The Magnificent Mind-Set Man is about gaining the physical, spiritual, intellectual, and emotional commitment and insatiable desire to adjust your thoughts, habits, and total attention to achieve ultimate success as you define it. The concepts taught herein will give you the sense and realization of a divine empowerment that is within you, which will help you find the selfdetermination to become the person you want to be.

You can, in fact, become a Magnificent Mind-Set Man or Woman in your own right. Just never give up, applying the Seven Transcending Mind-Sets of Success along the way of your own magnificent journey into your own Bokan Mountain.

www.ingramcontent.com/pod-product-compliance
Lightning Source LLC
LaVergne TN
LVHW041941070526
838199LV00051BA/2862